"Jedi's fine," she said, drawing the dog's gaze up to her, his nose nudging her leg as he heard his name.

"See, he knows it already," he told her, like he could somehow take credit for that.

She nodded, her gaze colliding head-on with Greg's when they both looked up from the dog at the same time. Like cars with locked bumpers, they stood there, blue eyes hooked to green, as though neither of them knew how to get them apart.

A prod at his thigh pulled Greg's attention a bit, but it wasn't until Wendy stepped back, and he glanced down to see that the dog had insinuated himself between them, that he finally escaped the woman's allure.

Saved by the dog.

And Greg wondered, as he said good-night, if he was there to teach Jedi or if the dog was there to teach him.

Either way, lesson learned.

He had to make certain that, over the next weeks of helping train a service dog, he kept his distance from Jedi's foster caregiver.

Dear Reader,

I'm so excited for you to meet Jedi! And Wendy and Greg, too, of course! My time spent in Spring Forest was fun and rewarding, but more, I felt hope here, and I hope you do, too. Hope for the future, whatever it might be. Whether it looks like you think it should or looks entirely different than you planned, you never know what good might roll in with tomorrow. Spring Forest, Jedi, Greg and Wendy reminded me of these things. And through them, I bequeath these same hopes to you.

And...if after reading this book, you want to find some Jedi type of love for your own life, I hope you'll look into local rescue organizations. I'd never opened my mind to that particular possibility, always buying my fur family members from breeders, until we passed by a window on our way to get a Christmas tree, saw big brown eyes, went inside, and our Jerry found us.

He was malnourished, had eating and drinking disorders, mites and internal parasites, and backed away if you approached him. We had a little girl fur family member at home. Had no plans to get another. But we took Jerry home that day, and fourteen years later, he's lying right beside me as I type this, because by my side is where he chooses to live. It took me a while (weeks) on the floor on my belly back then to get him to let me get close, and now my boy looks at me and wags his tail every single time I touch him. And his love...it has brought me through, held me up, during some of my darkest days. A miracle of love happened that day we'd thought we were only getting a tree. Which gives me hope for every single tomorrow.

I hope you enjoy *Love off the Leash*! You can find all of my socials, sales, news and giveaways, and a newsletter sign-up form at www.tarataylorquinn.com.

Tara Taylor Quinn

Love off the Leash

—

TARA TAYLOR QUINN

HARLEQUIN

SPECIAL
EDITION

Special thanks and acknowledgment are given
to Tara Taylor Quinn for her contribution
to the Furever Yours miniseries.

HARLEQUIN®

SPECIAL EDITION™

PLEASE RECYCLE
THIS PRODUCT IS RECYCLABLE

Recycling programs
for this product may
not exist in your area.

ISBN-13: 978-1-335-40862-4

Love off the Leash

Copyright © 2022 by Harlequin Enterprises ULC

For questions and comments about the quality of this book,
please contact us at CustomerService@Harlequin.com.

Harlequin Enterprises ULC
22 Adelaide St. West, 41st Floor
Toronto, Ontario M5H 4E3, Canada
www.Harlequin.com

Printed in U.S.A.

Having written over ninety novels, **Tara Taylor Quinn** is a *USA TODAY* bestselling author with more than seven million copies sold. She is known for delivering intense, emotional fiction. Tara is a past president of Romance Writers of America and a seven-time RITA® Award finalist. She has also appeared on TV across the country, including *CBS Sunday Morning*. She supports the National Domestic Violence Hotline. If you need help, please contact 1-800-799-7233.

Books by Tara Taylor Quinn

Harlequin Special Edition

Sierra's Web

His Lost and Found Family
Reluctant Roommates

The Parent Portal

Having the Soldier's Baby
A Baby Affair
Her Motherhood Wish
A Mother's Secrets
The Child Who Changed Them
Their Second-Chance Baby
Her Christmas Future

The Daycare Chronicles

Her Lost and Found Baby
An Unexpected Christmas Baby
The Baby Arrangement

The Fortunes of Texas

Fortune's Christmas Baby

Visit the Author Profile page
at Harlequin.com for more titles.

For my dearest, sweet Jerry Lee,
who taught me that being loved is not something
to take for granted, but rather that being loved is
something for which to be grateful. I thought that
we rescued you, but in reality, you rescued me.

Chapter One

"Six months, Papa? The cruise is six months long?" Meaning he'd be gone for Thanksgiving? And maybe Christmas, too? Wendy Alvarez was used to her father not being present in her life all that often—but this seemed a little extreme, even for him.

"We're going around the world..." As if that made his lengthy absence any less...impactful. It wasn't like she expected much from him—or they expected much from each other. After their family had fallen apart years before, the two of them had struggled to connect. It wasn't that she didn't want to be close—in fact, she wanted nothing more than to feel that sense of love, support and belonging that she'd had as a child before everything had gone wrong. But there was no getting that back. Just like there was no getting her brother or her mother back.

In the aftermath of everything, she had chosen to leave Raleigh, where she'd been born and raised and her father still had a home, to set up her accounting practice in the smaller suburban town of Spring Forest on the outskirts of the metropolis. Meanwhile, her father had remarried and started taking cruises. Any cruise. All-the-time cruises, like he was searching for those missing parts of himself in every port he could find. She tried to respect his right to mourn as he saw fit. But the timing of this particular cruise still hurt. He was the only family she had left, and they'd always been together for at least a little bit on holidays.

Lifting her satchel to her shoulder, she locked up her one room rented office downtown and headed out to her vehicle.

"I've got an appointment…on my way now, actually…" she said as the hands-free system in her SUV picked up. "But I can leave right after that, meet you for dinner, at least, before you go." Pushing him to make time for her was her role in their relationship. That, and choking back a boatload of hurt and insecurity.

Would she ever grow out of being the adolescent who'd felt like she wasn't enough yet and who was trying to hold them all together?

"Ah, *hija mia*, I'd love to do that, but we're meeting with the couple who'll be staying at our place while we're gone and then heading to an airport hotel room and a pre-cruise reception with a group of friends before an early night. We fly out to Florida before dawn."

And if she hadn't called to check in? Would he even have sent a text to let her know he was leaving the country?

Hija mia. Daughter mine. Toying with the tail of her braid pulled over her shoulder, she pulled out of the parking lot.

Of course, he would have sent a text. At some point along his journey. He'd send cool pictures now and then too, as he did on all of his cruises. He didn't forget her, he just…didn't remember her very often.

"How about a cup of coffee, then?" she asked. "I can be there by one thirty."

"I'd be too rushed," Steve Alvarez replied with his usual calm, steady manner. "No point in you dealing with all the city traffic, giving up your day, to see me for ten distracted minutes…"

She'd make the drive for a meeting of the eyes and a thirty-second hug. But, of course, she would never say so. The sense of connection she craved seemed to be something he actively avoided. In fact, it felt to her that he seemed to avoid feeling much of anything these days.

"We'll do something when I get back," Steve said, dropping into her silence.

The air in her car was the only audience to the

nod she gave. If her father said they'd do something, they would.

And she was lucky to have him. Michael was gone. And then Mama...

"Be safe, Papa."

"You, too, *Princesa...*"

Princess. A nickname she didn't hear often. Hardly at all. One that had rolled off her father's tongue daily, it seemed to her, before their close, perfect family had imploded.

Princess. She was no princess. More like a tall, curvy plain speaker who had more adopted family than she'd ever dreamed she could have. That was where she found her joy—and that was where she turned her thoughts when the pain of the past surged again.

Thinking of the dog she was about to pick up from Furever Paws Animal Rescue and deliver to the sexy Pilots for Paws pilot, Greg Martin, Wendy threw the tail of her dark French braid over her shoulder and signaled her turn.

While bookkeeping kept her bills paid, her real passion was her volunteer work with Pets for Vets, and it was always a good day when she had another dog ready to help a veteran in need. The fact that this dog was a rescue just made the sense of satisfaction that much stronger. It all went to reinforce her conviction that she was exactly where she was supposed to be, doing exactly what she was supposed to do.

Women weren't meant to stay home with their

parents and brothers forever. They were meant to grow up and make lives of their own.

It was high time she gave herself credit for doing just that.

Time she focused fully on the life she loved. The life she'd provided for herself, all on her own.

She wasn't fourteen anymore, idolizing her strong and dependable older brother. Being coddled by parents who spoiled her.

She was thirty-three. An accountant and book-keeper with her own successful business, in a town that had become dear to her. A town filled with people who knew her, who cared, who called and stopped by her office and needed her. A town filled with people she loved.

Her father leaving her to fend for herself over the holidays was a sign.

Moving on wasn't enough. It was time to finally, fully let go of who she'd been. Maybe then, she'd finally feel complete.

Anticipation powered Greg Martin that late June Friday morning as he saw Wendy's SUV pull into the drive of the private airport and head past the main lot toward his hangar. He might only be a volunteer with the completely volunteer-run Pilots for Paws program—transporting animals, free of charge, from shelters to their new homes—but the work was important, and a day with worthwhile reason to get up in the morning was a good day.

A day with flying on the schedule was even better. Greg was never happier than when he was in the air.

And a minute or two of meaningless flirting with the Pets for Vets volunteer as they did the potential new service-dog pass off was just…a welcome bonus.

"You party too hard last night, Martin?" she called out to him, the leashed Lab mix at her side keeping perfect pace with her, both of them making up for his slower pace that morning.

"You know it," he called back. He'd curse his stiff lower-left limb, but all the swearing in the world wouldn't get it back to what it once was. A surprise attack in Afghanistan had seen to that.

But he was alive. Doing what he loved most— flying.

"I get that that sexy butt of yours has the women chasing after you 24-7, but you could learn how to politely turn one or two of them down to keep them from running you quite so ragged, you know." She was grinning, her light green eyes sparkling with sass as her long legs caught up to him.

He hadn't had a date or been to any kind of real party in months. Just wasn't feeling it. But there was no harm in pretending. Flirting with Wendy made him feel like the man he used to be, at least for a little while. "I could, but…why?" Holding her gaze, he dared her to offer to show him why.

Knew she wouldn't.

Wished she would.

And wondered, not for the first time, if the tall, curvy accountant was seeing anyone.

Figuring that one for a definite yes.

Wendy, a gorgeous Latina, downplayed her looks with her serviceable clothes, braided hair and lack of makeup on that warm olive skin, but any heterosexual guy with blood in his veins would definitely look twice. At least.

He reached for the leash. She held on, saying, "I'll walk her to the plane."

If he'd had a better night, he probably would have held his tongue. But he hadn't, and he didn't. "What the hell for?"

"She's never flown. She could refuse to jump up—"

"Then, I'll lift her onto the plane. Put her in the kennel." He'd done it a dozen times before. Usually with his leg having a better day.

Chin up, she met his gaze. "And if she gets away and runs off?" The question was challenging, not the least bit sympathetic.

"I'll run after her," he stated unequivocally, chin just as high. It would hurt like hell, but while he'd never win another track meet, he'd get the job done, same as always.

Her look assessed him for a long few seconds more, but then she silently handed over the leash.

As he watched her walk away, he mentally kicked himself for his stubbornness. What would have been so bad about having her walk the dog to the plane?

It would have meant he could enjoy her company for a little longer, and that could only ever be a good thing. But no, his pride had to get involved at the idea that there was something about the situation that he couldn't handle on his own, leading him to cut their moment short. Anything to avoid even a moment where she might look at him with pity.

He had no idea what, if anything, she'd heard about him—other than the fact that he was an army vet. His creds were part of his volunteer bio. But if she'd been exposed to hearsay originating from his mother or sisters, he didn't want to know. There was such a thing as suffocating a guy with well-meaning nurturing.

And because suffocating wasn't on his agenda for the day, Greg put thoughts of his mother and siblings, of his battle-fueled nightmares and subsequent aching leg, firmly out of mind as he took to the skies, heading north. As always, the open sky greeted him like the best friend it was, and with a lighter heart he delivered frequent trip updates to the sweet young canine riding nervously behind him, letting her know she wasn't alone. Telling her, by the easy tone of his voice, that all was well.

He'd once thought the point of his life was to serve and protect in the military. A medical discharge had changed that plan.

And so he had found a new one.

To serve and comfort.

Not to *be* comforted. Or coddled. There were too

many other people, far worse off than he was, who really needed that kind of thing.

Like the blinded soldier who was waiting for this particular young Lab who'd not only be a faithful companion to him but as a guide dog would give him back some measure of personal freedom, as well. The landing and delivery went well, filling him with a sense of satisfaction that buoyed him along as he started the preparations for the trip home. Unfortunately, that feeling didn't last.

When he was busy and focused, he could manage to keep his nightmares at bay. But they always found him in the end. The previous night had been particularly bad, leaving him tired and out of sorts. So when he got the news that the weather report was predicting a storm in his returning flight path, it felt like just another kick when he was already down. This night of all nights, he did not want to have to deal with sleeping somewhere unfamiliar, somewhere where others nearby might hear him if he yelled.

And that meant staying up north to wait out a storm wasn't an option he was willing to consider. He needed a good night's rest, and the chances of that happening were much greater if he was in his own space. His own bed.

More importantly, if the horror flicks in his head continued a second night in a row, he'd be safely ensconced in his large home surrounded by his ten acres of wooded privacy, and no one would be the wiser.

He'd flown in major storms, was confident in his ability to handle the aircraft that was more family than personal possession to him. And did just fine right up until he was ten minutes from the private airport near Spring Forest. That was when the storm hit, with a much larger force than he had expected. The winds, rain and jagged lightning took on lives of their own. Not only did they blind and deafen him with their violent battering, they cut him off from nearby towers, destroying his ability to communicate with anyone who could guide him in.

Cut off and alone, the nightmares took hold of him, just as they did most nights. Imaginary voices, sometimes snippets from real people he'd known in the past, invaded his mind and turned his awareness into reels of torture.

Red haze blinded his gaze for a split second, followed by a gray that signaled nothingness. His chest constricted, stifling air intake while his stomach tightened to the point of pain. For a second. Until Greg took over.

"It's only panic," he said aloud. And the debilitating sense of doom dissipated, no opponent to his hard-won sense of self-control, to his determination to face his enemies head-on.

He could breathe again.

But that didn't come close to solving all of his problems. He still couldn't see past the controls directly in front of him. Or hear anything but a loud rumbling—a concoction of engine, thunder, rain, wind...

Then he saw everything. For a split second, the world around him was a stage of light, showing him the emptiness outside and the drenched land below. A loud crack sounded, like a gun going off next to his head. The plane rocked.

And he knew he'd been hit.

Not by opposing weaponry but by lightning. He was going down.

But he still had some control of the plane.

The plane. His salvation. He had to save his plane. That surety brought a new measure of calm, a deeper level of focus, and he visualized the brief glimpse of ground the flash of damaging light had given him.

Knew exactly where he was from the dozens of times he'd flown the route. Knew he couldn't reach his private landing strip near Hendrix, which was still several miles away, but there was another option—one that just might work. He calculated his speed with miles on the ground, and it just came to him where he had to land. An abandoned drive-in movie theater not far from Spring Forest. The place had a long driveway for moviegoers to wait in line to pay the entrance fee. The speakers and screens had long since been taken down, stolen, destroyed or salvaged, but that driveway was still there.

Without further consideration or question, he watched his gauges, determining how quickly he was losing height and how far he had to push to get himself in place. When he and his plane were alone in the air, people on the ground were his first concern, always. And then the plane.

The movie theater provided a way to save both.

So he would make it happen.

His neck jolted as the small aircraft hit turbulence and he rode the rough air like a motorboat on waves. Facing his challenge head-on. Sitting tightly as his small craft tossed violently.

Fully focused on the end in mind.

Had he not been watching the dials in front of him, he'd have been shocked at the first sight of the ground coming up to greet him out of the gloom— less than ten feet away. He missed the drive, clipped a tree he didn't remember being there, damaged a wing on a lone metal pole left standing and, as he touched down hard, slammed on the brakes in just enough time to prevent himself from sliding into the woods. The plane lurched hard, and his head cracked into the side panel beside him.

Greg's body bumped and slammed against the seat restraints holding him in place, his ears rang with internal sirens and then…everything was still.

Chapter Two

She was not going to text Greg Martin. He was a big boy. A professional pilot who'd been flying without her worry, or knowledge, long before he'd started volunteering to transport her dogs.

Thunder cracked and followed with a rumble that seemed to shake her house. Still, if Greg was in the air, it was because he was doing a favor for her. If he'd been caught in the storm…she couldn't help feeling like she was largely to blame.

Wasn't it just responsible of her to text and make sure he'd landed safely? Or had stayed up north for the night?

Had he ever flown through such bad weather on her behalf before? Looking back over the three years or more that he'd been flying her Pets for Vets animals around the region, who could remember for sure?

She was positive she'd never texted before to make sure he'd landed safely.

And there was her answer.

She'd had a bad morning—made better by a few minutes of seeing him. Teasing with him. The flirtation meant nothing. Greg, a man women drooled over, was a confirmed bachelor. Which made flirting with him safe. Fun, even.

But more than that, being with him that morning had helped put her world in perspective. Her father represented the child she'd been. Greg was a part of the life of the woman she'd become. A friend. Being with him for those few minutes that morning had turned her rotten mood completely around. Helping her realize that she was in the right place doing the right things for her.

Of course Greg was on her mind. He'd been the brightest part of her day.

But that was no cause to suddenly turn into a ninny and call him. He didn't know he'd helped her feel good about her life and her choices. Didn't need to know he'd helped.

Him knowing would ruin things, and she liked them exactly as they were.

Unspoken friends for however long they happened to be in each other's spheres.

No pressure.

No built-up expectations that could lead to letting each other down.

A text would have been an intrusion…certainly a massive protocol change…maybe even one requiring explanation.

Good call not to text.

Solidly decided.

No more contemplation.

Feeling calmer with her choice-making firmly behind her, Wendy slipped her phone into the back pocket of her lightweight chinos and headed down the hall to her home office and the satchel of files she'd brought from work.

But then her phone started ringing. That in itself wasn't strange. She might live by herself, but she rarely spent an entire evening in her own company. But when she pulled the cell from her pocket and got a glimpse at the caller ID, her heart started to pound.

Greg.

"Hello?"

She should have texted. She should have texted. She should have texted. Why hadn't she trusted her judgment?

"Hey."

Some of the anxiety twisting her stomach into knots eased after hearing his voice. He was obviously on the ground.

And sounded fine.

So wait—why the hell was he calling?

Did he want to screw things up between them?

Horror of horrors, had he somehow read more into her teasing that morning than had been there?

Trying to breathe while running a rapid and somewhat sketchy replay of the morning's conversation through her brain, she barely deciphered him saying, "You busy?" Did something about him sound off? Or was it just her who was flipping out over a phone call?

"Just home working. What's up?"

Maybe the call was related to their shared volunteer work. If he'd heard of another dog in need of help during his drop-off, she'd gladly help place him. Or her.

"I'm stranded," he told her. "You're the only person I know nearby." She'd been right about him not sounding quite right.

She swallowed with difficulty. "Stranded?"

Her intuition had been screaming at her. Why in the hell hadn't she listened?

"You know the old drive-in outside of town?"

"Town? My town? Spring Forest?" He'd only touched down at the local private airpark to pick up the Lab he'd been delivering for her. He'd have no reason to be in Spring Forest that night...

"I got struck by lightning and had to bring her down. I'm fine, but the plane's got some damage. I've already called air traffic control and local police. They told me that the plane's fine where it is until tomorrow, but I need a ride, and you're the only one I know in the area..."

He knew Birdie and Bunny, unlikely matriarchs in Spring Forest and the founders of the Furever Paws Animal Rescue that provided most of the animals that he transported; they were old friends of his mother's. But Wendy was *his* friend. She made the silent translation with growing warmth, in conjunction with the frown that was getting more pronounced.

"You don't sound fine. You sure you're okay?"

"Positive. I'm a trained fighter pilot, I know how to self-triage. I just need a ride. Unless you're occupied, I can…"

"…I'm on my way," she interrupted, already on her way out the door, keys in hand. "And you can self-triage to know if your eyes are dilated?" She wasn't a medical person, wasn't completely sure what signs to look for. "Seriously, I can call an ambulance. I do their books, and the EMT on duty tonight is the best—"

She heard him curse under his breath before he spoke again. "I don't need a damned ambulance, and if you call one, I'll call a cab. Which, you know, is what I should have done in the first place. I don't know what I was thinking, and I apologize for bothering you—"

"No! It's no bother. I'm glad you called, and I'm already headed your way." As she climbed into the car, she switched to the vehicle's Bluetooth system.

No cabs. The man had enough money to take one all the way to Hendrix. And then, without being checked out, he'd be rambling about, all alone on that big wooded property he talked about. He might claim that he didn't need an ambulance, but she couldn't imagine landing a plane after a lightning strike—without a proper runway—had been totally smooth and consequence-free. Whether he was willing to admit it or not, she was sure he'd acquired some injuries. If nothing else, it sounded like the kind of terrifying experience that could mentally and emotionally rattle even the steadiest of men. She didn't like the thought of him being alone after something like that.

And when he'd needed someone, he'd called her.

Which sent unfamiliar warm jolts through her.

Food for thought.

But first, she had to make sure Greg Martin was safe and as fine as he claimed he was.

If not for her—the errand he'd been running for her—he wouldn't have been up in the storm.

She owed him.

"I'm sorry for the inconvenience." Greg had the words ready and was delivering them as he opened the passenger door of Wendy's SUV and slid onto the roomy—even with his broad shoulders—seat. She'd barely brought the vehicle to a stop. The rain had stopped for the moment, and he'd jumped down out of the plane's cockpit the second he'd seen her headlights coming up the drive.

"You were holding your head all the way to the car. What's wrong?"

"Your headlights were blinding me." He could

hear that he sounded a little defensive, but he didn't like the evaluating tone in her voice. He was fine. He just maybe had the beginnings of a tension headache. He wasn't a headache kind of guy, thank God, but he could feel the tightness coming up through his neck. Nothing a hot shower couldn't fix.

He could see starlike glints in her eyes as she studied him in a darkness lit only by the vehicle's interior dashboard. "They weren't shining directly on you. Did you hit your head?"

The way she was peering at him, like she was looking for signs of something wrong, had him turning his head away and sitting up straight as he said, "I bumped a lot of things," in a lackadaisical tone. "You don't bring a craft down in a major storm without significant turbulence." There was nothing to worry about. He knew what serious injury felt like, and what he was experiencing wasn't it. Not even close.

"Greg, come on. Did you bump your head?"

The emphatic tone to her voice, coupled with the lack of her foot on the gas needed to power the vehicle, had him thinking back. "Yeah," he admitted. "When I landed. It bumped the side panel—but not very hard." He felt the spot. "There's not even a lump."

She continued to watch him.

"You want to feel?" he asked, not flirting, but close, hoping that would rattle her enough to get her to back off. He knew she liked the playful, flirtatious vibe between the two of them, but only if he kept it very light. Anything that smacked of real intimacy she tended to avoid.

The question worked. She put the vehicle in motion. Turned toward town, not the highway and thirty-plus miles down the road where his own vehicle awaited in the garage on his property. Exactly as he'd expected. He didn't mind: he'd never had any intention of asking her to drive him all the way home. No way he wanted to be responsible for her driving back from Hendrix alone late at night in the rain.

"If you just drop me at the nearest gas station, I'll call a cab where I can wait inside out of the rain."

"I'll make a deal with you."

The night had pretty much sucked. He wasn't in a mood for bargaining. "I'm not aware that I'm in need of any deal." He was a free man who'd called a friend for a ride. Period. He had other options.

"I'll quit worrying about whether or not my favor inadvertently caused you physical damage and quit trying to figure out a way to get you medical attention if you'll agree to bed down at my place tonight."

A night in Wendy Alvarez's home? He was a little intrigued. Enough to give her deal some consideration.

Right up until he thought about the nightmares—the number one reason he never spent an entire night with a woman. Never let himself fall asleep after sex.

"I'd hate to cause you worry," he said slowly.

"You could have a concussion, Greg. I'm just being practical here."

His head didn't really hurt. Not badly. "I didn't lose consciousness."

"You think I have cooties or something?"

More like he did. "No."

"You called me, remember?"

Yeah, why had he done that? He'd still been on an adrenaline rush. Not a high. Just…a bit het up. And he'd thought of Wendy.

Because she was the only person nearby he considered a personal friend.

He'd reached out to a friend.

Completely atypical.

Still…he'd done it.

"Do you even have a guest room?"

"I have a really nice couch. And it's all yours for the night. Along with a wake-up call every two hours, house rules."

He didn't have a concussion. But if it would ease her worry…and more, if it would convince her to continue to call him every time she had a dog to transport up north…

"I left my go bag in the plane."

She pulled a quick U-turn and headed back down the road to the drive-in. And he didn't argue.

Chapter Three

Wendy didn't entertain at home. She was one person, so it usually ended up being much easier for others to have her over, especially her friends who had kids or pets they needed to be home with. Her house was on the outskirts of Spring Forest, kind of out of everyone's way, and she didn't mind being the one who did the driving back and forth. And her office in town was an open door with people stopping in often just to say hello.

The additional benefit of this was that her home got to feel like a private sanctuary. Peaceful and quiet and all hers.

And now, she'd invited Greg Martin to spend the night.

Because he'd flirted with her for a couple of minutes that morning and had inadvertently given her understanding that made her feel validated about her life?

Because Pets for Vets was the most important part of her life and he'd been hurt while working for them?

Whatever the reason, he was in her home now, and it was...weird. Those first hugely awkward moments of having Greg's six-foot-one broad-shouldered body taking up space in her private sphere unhinged her a bit. Made her nervous. Not in a scared way. In an extra-energy, clumsy way.

She told him to make himself at home but didn't show him past the kitchen door they'd come through from the garage.

"Can I get you something to drink?" she offered, opening the refrigerator. Her mother had always offered refreshment; she had been a great hostess. "And maybe something to eat? Did you get a chance to have dinner?"

"No," he admitted. "I was planning to eat when I got home. But I don't want you to go to any trouble—"

"No trouble at all," she insisted. "I have some leftover grilled chicken. It should make a pretty good sandwich." Without waiting for him to agree or argue, she pulled out the meat along with a loaf of bread, lettuce, tomato and condiments and began assembling a sandwich.

"I forget—did you say yes to something to drink?" she asked. She had beer, but she wasn't about to offer that to someone who had just hit his head. So non-alcoholic beverages it was. "I have water, orange juice, milk, soda, water, of course... Oh, I said that already, didn't I?"

Wendy knew she probably sounded silly, but she so badly wanted her place to seem comfortable and welcoming to Greg. She wanted him to want to be there.

"A glass of water would be great, thanks," he said, standing awkwardly by her counter.

"Feel free to sit down," she gestured toward the kitchen table and chairs, mentally wincing as she took in how plain and dinged-up the set looked. She'd bought them secondhand at a great price, figuring she hardly needed anything fancy or new when no one would be seeing her kitchen but her. And now Greg was here.

She knew there was no way on earth her house could even halfway live up to his own elegant home. Not that she'd ever been there. But Bunny and Birdie had told her that he'd inherited a lot of money from his grandparents and that his home was huge and lovely.

And that he rarely, if ever, had visitors. Like her.

"Here you go," she announced, bringing over the plated sandwich along with the water.

"Thank you." He didn't look at her, just grabbed the sandwich.

Leaving her with nothing to do but stand there watching him eat. She immediately started fidgeting. "I'll just...um...go set up the couch for you," she announced, scurrying out of the room like some kind of scared rabbit.

As she went to pull sheets out of the hall closet to cover the beige tweed couch she'd also purchased used, it occurred to her that she should have offered to take him home and insisted on keeping watch there.

It wouldn't have been nearly as...invasive...as that athletically perfect body taking up the entire expanse of cushion that she'd been known to sleep on herself when she wanted the television for company.

She could have watched over him at his house.

Why hadn't she thought of that?

Was it too late to suggest the idea?

Coming down the hall, she busily formed words to get them out of her house and back on track. Rejected her first couple of mental tries. And came to a stop as she reached the archway leading into the family room. Greg—shoes and belt off—was fully supine on the couch, eyes closed.

His go bag lay zipped under the table where he'd left his wallet, keys and belt.

He couldn't possibly be asleep. She'd been gone less than five minutes, and he'd only just started on his sandwich then.

Hadn't even, to her knowledge, used the restroom yet.

Had he fallen ill? Passed out? Was he succumbing to some internal injury from the crash? Heart pounding, she moved quietly closer, noticed his even breathing. "You okay?" she asked.

"Mmm-hmm." The response came immediately. Almost slumberously.

"I'll wake you in two hours," she said softly. She grabbed a sandwich for herself from the kitchen and took it and a glass of water down the hall to her bedroom, leaving the bottle of beer she'd have preferred in the refrigerator for a night when she wasn't on duty.

No way she was going to lower her inhibitions even a little bit when she had someone in her house to look after.

She texted her EMT client before she took her first bite. He answered all her questions, reassuring her that as long as Greg woke up for her and wasn't showing any other symptoms of physical distress, he likely was just fine.

She spent the next hour sitting up, fully clothed, on her bed, reading up on every cause of, sign of and potential remedies for concussion, anyway. Trying not to think about any muscle, tendon or organ trauma that Greg might have suffered, on her behalf, that night. Reminded herself that they likely had nothing to worry about.

Focusing on the medical side of things was...well, not comforting, exactly, but it was better than letting her mind wander in other directions. It mostly kept her from focusing on the fact that she had a man who had the power to change her mood, a man to whom she might be drawn, sleeping within her walls. His body, his heat, in direct physical contact with her couch cushions.

When she started thinking about their microscopic epithelial tissues comingling, she set her alarm, turned out the light and found an old G-rated family movie to stream quietly on her phone. And missed the opening credits, first scene, and probably the second, too, while she ran off in her head with visions of her sofa holding the man she'd have driven hours to rescue. And maybe wouldn't mind holding, too.

Just until she knew he was as well as he claimed.

Greg woke up just after ten. Lay in the dark in a room that wasn't familiar and yet didn't feel strange to him, either. He had to pee. Wanted to have a shower and brush his teeth.

On the other hand, he wanted to avoid contact with his hostess. The room, her home, the damned good sandwich…they were all mucking with him… with his vision of the role Wendy Alvarez played in his life. They were friends. Casual friends who could flirt with each other comfortably because they both knew it didn't mean anything. He couldn't want more.

He had no more to offer.

Sitting up, he took stock of his belongings. His gaze landed on the keys on the scarred wooden table.

If he had his truck, he'd just leave a note and go. But his truck was miles away. Like it or not, he was here for the night.

As he sat up and stretched, he winced. His stomach muscles felt a little tender…bracing against seatbelt trauma…and it seemed like he'd wrenched a muscle in his neck.

He needed a hot shower to loosen his muscles and wash the adrenaline-fueled sweat off of his skin.

When they'd first come inside, when she'd been fumbling around the kitchen and refusing to look at him, she'd mumbled something about the guest bathroom being the first hallway door on the left. It felt a little strange to help himself to a shower at someone else's house, but she'd told him to make himself at home. And anyway, maybe the shower was the best place for him to be.

If she had set her alarm—and he was certain she had—she'd be out in another ten minutes or so, just to make sure he woke up. If he was in the shower, he wouldn't have to face her when she came out to check on him.

He didn't want to see her. Not then. Not the way he was feeling. All cozy and yet…not.

Comfortable in her space, and not good with that.

Wide awake and wondering what kind of television she watched when she was home alone at night.

No, it would definitely be better if he was in the shower. That way, he could avoid seeing her. And she'd be reassured that he could, indeed, wake up. A perfect solution.

Plan approved, Greg was just turning on the shower when he heard an alarm go off in another room. Clicking the bathroom lock, just to ensure that there'd be no well-meaning head peeking in to check on him, he turned on the overhead exhaust fan, stripped down and let Wendy's hot water sluice over him.

Wide awake and still dressed, Wendy settled her head against her pillow, reset her alarm, placed the phone right next to her, closed her eyes and listened to the muted sounds of water spray coming from down the hall.

The man was naked in the shower she cleaned once a month to keep the dust off.

Was that what her life had become? Keeping the dust off unused parts?

She swallowed. Willed herself back to sleep. If she was asleep, two hours would pass quickly—and she'd have the rest she needed to deal with a busy day in the morning. She not only had a pile of work at the office, and a new client coming in who'd need full Saturday energy from her, but there was a shelter outside of Hendrix that had just taken in a young golden retriever that they were holding for Wendy.

And she could still hear the shower. He was taking a long one. Standing still under the spray?

Those long legs… She imagined them covered in

the dark hair that fell over his ears, the color of his shortly trimmed beard…and imagined other places where that dark hair might be found, too, before quickly moving her mental perusal up to the broad, athletic stomach and chest.

Fire slid down to her own private places and…

Stop.

Who was to say he wanted her that way, regardless? He could have his pick—and there was no reason to believe she'd make the mark.

The bathroom door clicked open, and Wendy quietly turned on the family movie she'd been streaming and forced herself to focus on the story. Her chances of falling asleep were pretty much nil, but she could at least rest.

She wasn't even aware of when she drifted off. But she was very aware of when she woke up.

"Ahhhg!" Wendy sat straight up. Heart pounding, she slid into awareness, trying to decipher reality from dream. Something had woken her—something startling. But what?

"Ahhhnnng!" As the agonizing sound rent the house a second time, she flew out of bed and down the hall.

Rounding the arch into the family room, catching her shoulder on the rounded drywall, she frantically focused through the shadows to the form lying on her couch. He lay there, completely still.

Oh, God. What if it was a medical emergency? A

ruptured kidney, a brain bleed… One awful possibility after another raced through her mind.

"Ahg!" The animallike noise came again as Greg rolled, throwing an arm onto the back of the couch.

His pain stifled the air in the room, making breathing difficult. She had to help him.

To get help.

Eyeing his phone on the table, she reached for it and jumped when a vise formed around her wrist. The grip was not painfully tight—at least not as long as she wasn't moving—but definitely steel-like.

"Greg?"

The word wasn't even fully spoken before the fingers snatched away from her wrist, leaving her with an odd realization. Her skin, where he'd touched her, was wet.

Not moving closer but not leaving, either, she called his name a second time. "Greg?"

"Yeah."

"You're in pain."

"I'm fine."

Was he trying to insult her intelligence? She was filled with a combination of worry, compassion, sympathy…and anger? She pulled on the latter to combat the weakening effects of the other three.

"You're not fine, Greg. You're in pain. Hollering out with it in your sleep…" Growing stronger as she spoke, more determined, she approached the couch, sat on the end by his feet and faced him in the near darkness.

He'd lifted his head up onto the arm of the couch. He was breathing hard, as though he'd been running. In the moon's timid light, she could see a sheen of sweat on his face.

Her wet skin beneath his hand...the man was feverish.

"I'm calling an ambulance."

"No!" The volume with which the one word came at her might have given her pause if she was at all afraid of the man from whom it had been wrung. If Greg had meant to hurt her, her wrist would be bruised.

She glanced at the hand that had grasped her and saw how badly it was shaking.

"Greg, please. I don't know why you're so opposed to medical treatment, but with the amount of pain you seem to be in, you could have a brain bleed. Or internal injury from the seat restraints in the cockpit. Look at you—you're feverish, shaking..."

Hoisting himself up farther into the corner of the couch, pulling his feet farther away from her thighs, he sighed, somewhat heavily. "I just... I had a nightmare, okay? I fell asleep too soon after the less-than-stellar landing, and I was just dreaming. It happens. I apologize for waking you."

She weighed his words carefully, trying to figure out if he was just being macho. But he didn't sound like he was wracked with pain. On the contrary, his shaking hand aside, he seemed quite calm.

Which calmed her.

Maybe it helped that she'd had some experience with being wrenched from sleep by another's nightmares. Her brother, Michael, had slept in the room right next to hers.

Without saying another word, she got up, went to the kitchen, poured a cup of milk, warmed it in the microwave and carried it back to him. "This might help," she said.

It had usually helped Michael, but then he'd been a milkaholic.

"Thank you." Greg took the glass, emptied it and leaned his head back against the couch.

"You okay now?"

"I'm—"

"Fine…" she finished for him. "I know."

"I'm sorry I woke you. Seriously."

She nodded. "I'm guessing we probably don't have to get up again in two hours," she said, heading for the hall. "We could both use some sleep." She didn't expect a response.

Didn't need one.

What she did require was some time to assimilate all of her thoughts. Her realizations that day… that Greg had been the one to help her over the final moments of letting the past go…and that he'd then had a nightmare in her home, waking her as Michael had… It was like fate was having a laugh at her expense. He'd helped her feel free from her past in the morning, and that night had brought it clearly back to her, too—yelling out in pain as Michael had.

"Wendy?" The soft male voice sent tingles all the way through her.

And that, too. Her body's reaction to him, the emotions he was raising in her, all of a sudden. It wasn't like they'd just met or something…"Yeah?"

"Thank you."

"Anytime, Martin, anytime," she said lightly but, unlike earlier, when she reached her bedroom, she closed the door behind her.

Like Michael, he'd just lied to her. Telling her he was fine. Shutting her out.

Didn't matter if she wanted to help him or not. He wasn't going to let her.

And at the moment, she was too weary to fight him.

Chapter Four

Greg was up, teeth brushed and ready for the day when Wendy came out of her bedroom a few hours later. She'd showered. Not only had he heard the water going, but her hair, already in a tight French braid, was still wet. Wearing another pair of the lightweight cotton pants he always saw her in, paired with a sleeveless white V-neck blouse, she gave him the sense that she was all business and ready to get on with it.

He gratefully accepted the message. After all, it wasn't as if he wanted to have a long, emotional talk about his nightmare or what a mess he'd been in its aftermath. All business was definitely the way to go.

Only later, when he was riding in the cab of the truck he'd hired to tow his plane, did he allow himself to acknowledge that he maybe harbored a bit of regret that he and Wendy hadn't made some kind of plan to be in contact, or something. Which made no sense. Their paths would cross again soon, as they always did, to transport dogs, but there was no real way of knowing when. And no reason for him to suddenly want to know when.

Despite her absence, he continued to think about her over the next couple of days.

It had been years since he'd spent the night with anyone else in the same quarters. Even when he flew out to Arizona to see his parents, who'd retired in the desert to enjoy year-round blue skies, sunshine and warmth, he bunked in a nearby hotel room rather than the spare bedroom in their home.

It had been almost nice, sharing her space, until the nightmare ruined it. Holy bad timing on that one. Kind of pissed him off. Like his damned consciousness couldn't let him just have a feel-good moment? She'd thought he'd been in physical pain and he'd just been reliving a hellacious memory in his sleep. Keeping it alive, even subconsciously, so he never forgot the men who'd died. Never forgot that he owed them. In retrospect, it was probably good to have some time before he saw her again.

There were some things in life that doctors couldn't fix. Some aches that medicine couldn't dissipate. No matter how brilliant the doctor or advanced the medical technology. And when it came to those problems, the ones a guy just had to accept, the only way to deal with the situation was to keep himself away from others and keep his defenses strong against letting anyone in.

And yet, when Birdie and Bunny Whitaker called on Monday, saying they had a couple of home-cooked meals to bring by for him, he didn't demur.

Not even a little bit. Word of his emergency landing had gotten out. He'd been touted for his masterful handling of the small aircraft, bringing it down without hitting power lines, homes or busy roads. The locals were grateful for his care and his skill— and they were also concerned about how he was in the aftermath. And if the Whitaker sisters didn't get eyes on him personally, his mother would, no doubt, catch the next plane out of Phoenix.

And she'd have his own pair of sisters driving up from Charlotte to sit vigil until she arrived, their professional jobs and personal relationships be damned. He'd be drowning in endlessly doting relatives before he knew it.

Still, as he heard the bell ring on his oversize front door and made his way across the porcelain floor toward it, he was filled with as much grateful understanding as anything.

He had family he loved who loved him back.

And that was, overall, a very good thing. Even if he did get along with them better from afar.

Besides, the quirky, sixtysomething, never-married Whitaker sisters were entertainment in their own right. Birdie, the older of the two by one year, the taller of the pair and the practical outspoken one, still didn't eclipse her shorter, plumper dreamer of a younger sister. The duo, one mouthy and one less, back living together for the time being in the rambling old house they'd inherited, had been an unspoken source of good-natured amusement to him as a teen. His mother, with her various volunteer meetings, would fill the house with women, and he'd mostly make himself scarce. Except when the Whitaker sisters were over. He'd liked them.

Now they marched right in, Birdie first, and headed straight for his kitchen, as though they owned the place. They'd been there before, when his folks had visited from Phoenix and his mother had invited them over. His parents had stayed in the guest wing of the house, one with its own entrance and small living quarters, completely separate from his own wing, and yet his mother had made her presence known all over the house with little touches—a set of curtains here, a new throw rug there.

"You've got baked ziti with salad and a pot roast for your main courses," Birdie said as she placed them in his well-stocked refrigerator.

"Heating directions are here on the top," Bunny added, pointing to the cards taped to the top of the foil-covered pans she carried. "And I made chicken noodle soup, too, because, well, you know, it's supposed to cure everything."

While Birdie was in better physical shape than her younger sister, Bunny was the one who colored all of the gray out of her brown hair. She deposited her goods on the top shelf that Birdie had just cleared and then said, "I need to use the ladies' room. The drive out here was longer than I remembered," and off she went.

"How are you feeling?" Birdie eyed him up and down, right there in the middle of his kitchen.

"Fine."

Eyes narrowing, she gave him another once-over. "You sure about that?"

"I am."

"Look me straight in the eye and tell me that nothing hurts."

He looked. "My leg is a little stiff. Nothing else hurts."

Lips pursed as she considered that, weighing his words, she nodded. "You still have some of the liniment Bunny made for you?"

"Yes."

"You using it?"

"Actually, I am."

"Good. Your mom said your plane is fixable?"

"Already done," he told her. "She's being transported to her hangar this morning." It had cost him a bit—even with doing part of the work himself—but any price was worth it. The plane, flying, him being in the sky was his life.

And he had the money.

"It was horrifying to her, being so far away when

she heard about what happened. She was quite beside herself, I can tell you—"

He nodded. "I know. And…thanks for the dinners. They will be very appreciated." He meant every word. The sisters could cook almost as well as his mother.

Glancing toward the dining room, through which Bunny had disappeared, Birdie asked, "Did your mother tell you I have a plan to get Bunny back with Stew Redmond?"

She hadn't, in fact, but Greg knew about the saga of Bunny's relationship, from the surprising reveal that Bunny had an online boyfriend to the amazement everyone had felt when Bunny had left town to go traveling with him in an RV and all the way to the shocking return of Bunny not so long ago, noticeably without her beau. The whole thing had everyone riveted, like it was a soap opera.

Of course, the whole town loved Bunny and Birdie—they were Spring Forest institutions and two of the kindest women in the world—but the fact that they *were* such institutions and that they'd been fully focused on running the Furever Paws Animal Rescue together for so many years meant that no one had expected anything about their lives to ever change. Bunny's romance with Stew had been entirely unexpected, just like Birdie's own romance with the town's retired vet, Doc J. Everyone was rooting for both of those relationships to succeed.

Which was why everyone was so sad that both relationships were currently on the rocks. Bunny had returned without Stew, and Birdie and Doc J. had had a fight that ended in the doctor heading off to Florida alone when Birdie refused to leave with him. Greg hoped they were able to work things out. And he really, really hoped that they were able to do that while leaving him out of it. He had no desire to poke around in anyone's love life. People in glass houses shouldn't throw stones, after all.

Keeping his face serious as Birdie repeated her question, Greg shook his head a second time.

"Well, I'm not exactly sure how I'm going to make it work, but—" Birdie said, looking excited. But before she could divulge more, Bunny was back.

And when Birdie excused herself to the facilities, Bunny gave him her version of questions, checking up on him, wanting to know how scared he'd been, up in the storm, when he'd known his plane was going down. And how he'd been sleeping.

She was a little harder to fend off, claiming she could clearly see that he hadn't been sleeping much. He had no argument for that since it was true. He'd actively avoided sleep as a way to stave off the nightmares that were attacking in full force, but he managed to distract her with praises for her liniment, letting her know how much he'd been using it over the past few days.

She preened a bit. And then, glancing toward the dining room, said, "Did your mom tell you I have a plan to get Birdie and Doc J. back together?"

He gave her the truth. "She didn't."

"Well, I'm going to…" Her words dropped off abruptly as sounds of Birdie's return reached them.

He thought about offering to make coffee—something his mother had always done when she'd had ladies over—but his phone rang before he got the words out.

Wendy.

He hadn't heard from her since he'd left her home early Saturday morning.

Glancing from the screen back to the sisters, as he sent Wendy's call to voice mail, he told them that the call was business and that he needed to get back to work.

Thanks to his inheritance, he didn't have a regular day job, but on top of watching over his own investments, he managed a few nonprofits, which required hours in his home office pretty much every day. And while Pets for Vets and Pilots for Paws weren't charities, or programs he managed, he also treated his volunteer time with both as seriously as he would any job.

It took another ten minutes to get the ladies out the front door—they each mentioned, again, that he really should have a pet or two—and he, again, explained that his flying often took him away for long hours, sometimes overnight, which wouldn't be fair to any pet. Eventually, they said their goodbyes.

Their car wasn't even out of sight before he was

listening to Wendy's voice mail. "Hey, it's Wendy Alvarez. Call me."

The brief message told him nothing. Was her call about business? Pleasure?

Did he want to know?

Turned out, he did.

He called her while he waited at his hangar for his plane to arrive. The aircraft's safe-flight inspection was due to begin that afternoon, with a three-man crew, and he was eager to have the twenty- to fifty-hour process done. To know that he was free to fly once more.

"How are you?" she asked, right off.

"Fine."

"No residual effects from Friday night?"

"None." An honest answer. The intensity of his debilitating nightmares the past night or two had probably been partially triggered by the near crash he'd had, but the storm-induced emergency landing had certainly not been the cause of them.

He'd had one the night before he'd gone up on Friday, too.

"I'm not sure I believe you, but I'm glad to hear it," she said, a note of warmth translating over the wire to him. Whether she'd actually sent it or he'd heard it in there of his own accord, he didn't know.

"I have a potential flight coming up, Wednesday morning," she said, "and fully understand if you're not ready yet, but I didn't want to call anyone else without checking with you first."

This was normal protocol—her giving him the first shot at any flights Pets for Vets needed. Him working for free could be one of the reasons she did so, but he liked to think it was more than that. Regardless, he'd been grateful for the flight hours he logged helping her out. It was much more satisfying accomplishing something good and useful for another veteran than just going up and flying aimlessly to get his hours in. Plus, he liked being someone she could turn to.

He liked being needed.

Contributing.

And…she had a flight for Wednesday morning. He thought about going, expecting to feel the usual rush of happiness at the thought of being up in the air.

But instead, fear suffused his entire system. Weakening him. Bringing out an instant sweat, escalating his pulse. He felt nauseous, his heart pounding against his chest. It was like he was suffocating. He could barely hold the phone steady to his ear.

Then he took a breath. And another. Focused on relaxing his gut muscles, thought about Wendy's green eyes sparkling up at him in the sunshine.

And said, "I'm not sure the plane's going to be ready."

She was understanding about it, immediately offered to find someone else to do the flight and ended the call on a friendly note.

Greg heard her *Talk to you soon* even after she'd

clicked off. Dropped his hand and stared out at nothingness.

The thought of going up again, being up there... had brought a wave of panic so deep he'd almost passed out.

What the hell?

What the *hell*?

He was afraid to fly?

He bent at the waist as a new wave of pain hit his stomach, arms hanging down to the ground, and then squatted, before falling to his butt on the cement.

If he lost flying...

The one thing that made him forget the pain of living while other men had died...being up in the sky was the only time he still felt fully alive...

And that was gone?

Snatched away at the hands of a storm?

A different kind of storm than the barrage of gunfire that had come out of nowhere and taken out a quarter of his unit. Left some half-alive. Robbed him of his plan for a lifelong military career.

Was that life, then? A series of random storms that slowly took away parts of you until there was nothing left?

Emotion tightened the back of his throat.

Feeling desperate, he forced himself to think again about going up. Maybe it was a fluke, maybe he could push past the fear if he focused hard on what he loved. He imagined the rush as he gathered speed on the runway…and then he started to sweat, to shake.

Took a deep breath. Shuddered.

And buried his head between his knees.

Chapter Five

The second she hung up the phone, Wendy wanted to call Greg back. Something wasn't right with him. The certainty of that was so strong within her it scared her.

Going through the mail that had just been delivered through the slot in her office door, she tried to dismiss the sensation. While she'd known Greg for years, it wasn't like they'd ever done more than meet at airstrips for dog pass-offs. Why would she suddenly think that she had some kind of inside track to his deeper self? That kind of insight into him was something she just didn't have—nor was it something she wanted. Because even if the universe had taken some bizarre turn on her, she couldn't act upon any twinges that would lead her to a deeper relationship.

She just wasn't that woman.

Didn't want to be.

While she liked sex, she didn't want the emotional entanglement that inevitably wormed its way into the process. She wasn't built that way. The situation wouldn't end well.

Friendship was fine, but getting truly attached to and invested in someone would be setting herself up to get hurt. She'd learned that lesson from all the members of her family—from her brother and mother who were now gone, and from her father who seemed intent on running as far away from her as he could get.

And yet, after warring with herself for a day and a half, on Tuesday evening she parked her SUV at home, walked a quarter of a mile to the small pub she frequented often enough to know the waitstaff, grabbed the private corner table, ordered a beer and…called Greg.

She'd already finalized plans to pick up the golden retriever from a foster in the morning and deliver it to another pilot in Raleigh for a flight up north to the vet waiting for it. She didn't have a flight to offer Greg, and yet there she was, waiting for him to pick up.

Giving up on him after the sixth ring, she was moving her thumb to end the call rather than leave a voice mail, when he picked up.

"Hello." Just that. No acknowledgment that it was her on the line, though his caller ID would have told him so.

And there she sat, only one sip of beer down, with no idea what to say to him.

"Hi," she offered, for lack of anything else to say. He didn't reply, clearly waiting for her to explain why she had called.

"How are you?" she finally asked.

"Fine."

She was really starting to hate that word.

"And the plane?"

"Passed inspection."

Disappointment coursed through her. "So you could have taken tomorrow's flight."

"Yeah."

There didn't seem to be any regret in his tone that he'd missed out. So completely contrary to Greg's normal eagerness to take on every flight she had to give him.

Had she turned him off, commandeering him to stay with her? Crossed a line?

"Are you blowing me off?"

It might be for the best for her, personally.

But for the rescue dogs who found purpose and homes? The vets who benefited from them?

"No."

"Then, what?" They hadn't even established that there was a *what*.

"I might be getting in my own way."

She about dropped the phone. Paid attention to the bottle of beer she raised to her lips, holding it carefully as she drank.

Greg was admitting something personal to her. Giving her a chance to be something for him. Part of her—the part that studiously avoided intimacy—wanted to run away from it. But another part of her—the voice inside that had made her call him—wanted to help. She'd been right. Something wasn't right with him. Feeling certain that reaching out like this was very rare for him, she mostly wanted to be part of his support system.

It was Michael all over again—and so much more.

She couldn't mess it up.

"How so?"

"Coming down the other night...I panicked for a second."

The world stopped in place. Just held there while she processed the fact that Greg Martin had just shared a personal confidence with her.

And she wanted more.

"Only for a second?" she asked, somewhat cautiously. She wanted to encourage him to keep talking but not make it seem like she was steering the conversation or looking for a particular answer from him. This had to be hard for him to talk about. Her job, as she saw it, was to be quietly supportive and nonjudgmental.

"Yeah." He'd taken so long to answer, she'd been afraid he'd already clammed up on her.

"Okay." If he'd wanted her to be shocked, he was going to be disappointed.

"I got it together after that first second. Focused."

"And brought the plane down expertly." It was a fact. She felt like she should put it out there, remind him of his strength after he'd admitted a momentary weakness.

"That time. But what about the next?" He'd nearly whispered the question, as though he couldn't bear to hear it uttered.

"What about it?"

"I might be having difficulties with that."

Oh.

Oh, God.

Michael had gone away strong and sure. And come home afraid to stand in front of a window. Any window. He'd taken paths around them. Ducked beneath them.

She'd even seen him crawling beside the window seat in the dining room once. When he'd glanced up and realized she'd seen him, he'd looked so embarrassed.

Tough thing for a fourteen-year-old girl to witness in the big brother she idolized. She hadn't thought less of him for having new phobias. But it had broken her heart to see his shame, to know that he'd seen his behavior as evidence of a humiliating weakness rather than proof of a wound that needed time and care to heal. She'd wanted to help. Just hadn't known how.

She knew a lot more at thirty-three than she had at fourteen.

"I'm listening if you want to talk about them," she chose her words carefully, like walking on glass, afraid that Greg would clam up again.

It would be a lot harder to help him if she didn't know what they were dealing with.

"I might have had a moment or two of unease in the hangar."

Her heart dropped. He'd had a potentially fatal experience, after all. "Unease?" She wanted to be there with him. To understand. To help. To find out that she was imagining things to be worse than they were...

"I got cold sweats in the cockpit." The drop of his tone didn't hit with nearly as much impact as what she thought he was telling her.

"You went up?!" That had to be good. He was alive. Meant he'd made it back down, too.

"No."

Oh. A vision of him sitting in his plane in the hangar, struggling, made it impossible for her to swallow the sip of beer she'd just taken.

"I'm scared to go back up."

Swallowing the beer, feeling it go down like a big, painful lump, she wanted to spill platitudes and encouragement all over him. And knew she couldn't. They weren't what he needed.

Oh, God. What if he couldn't fly? She wouldn't blame him at all. But...he loved being in the air.

More than anything else she'd ever heard him talk about.

"Just for the moment," he added, talking faster with every word. "I'll get through it."

Denial wasn't an option—but pushing him might make him change the subject. Every word could be critical. "How do you know that?"

"Because no matter how much I sweat, I'm going back up. I'd rather die than be grounded. And no way I can fly while putting others in danger, so…I'll get through it. This is just another challenge. I've had others. And just like with those, I'll face it. And I'll beat it."

She believed him. Except that…he'd turned down a job.

"Did you know yesterday that your plane would probably be ready for tomorrow?"

"There was a good chance. Not a certainty."

"But you said no to the flight."

"I couldn't leave you in the lurch. In the event something didn't pass inspection." The answer came out smooth and automatic—almost like he'd prac- ticed it. Or maybe this was the excuse he'd been giv- ing himself to justify his actions?

He could have rented a plane. He'd done so once before, when a preflight check had shown a small repair needed on his own aircraft.

"I have a suggestion."

"I don't need any. I've got this. Seriously."

So why had he told her about it?

"You haven't heard my suggestion."

Taking his lack of response for acquiescence, she said, "You might try one of the Pets for Vets dogs. One that's trained to deal with anxiety."

"I'm trained to deal with it. And I did just fine." His tone bristled.

She'd pissed him off. Or at least raised a strong response in him.

"I'm only saying…it could help."

"I'm not into being dependent on others," he told her, and she had a feeling the message was directed at her as much as at the as-yet imaginary dog she'd suggested. "I help myself."

"I help myself, too, but no one can go through life totally alone."

"You seem to do a pretty good job of it."

The jab was low. Hit hard enough that she felt it.

"I try," she said, heading back to her corner to reassess.

"Yeah. Me, too."

But…she'd called him. He'd answered. Told her he was struggling.

"So where does that leave us?" she asked, viewing the trees and the neighborhood next to the pub. Taking a sip from her half-empty bottle of beer.

"Right where we've always been."

His response relieved her. She couldn't say why.

"You want me to call next time I need a pilot?"

"If you want."

If you want. Not *Of course.* He was leaving the ball in her court.

And the response she had for him was, "Talk soon, then."

"Yeah. And…thanks," he added right before clicking off.

Wendy had no idea what on earth he was thanking her for.

But his gratitude felt good.

Wednesday morning, just after dawn, Greg Wesley Martin presented himself to his airplane hangar. He'd inherited his backbone from his father, Randolph Wesley Martin, a retired career–army brigadier general, and his grandfather, William Wesley Martin, a career–army colonel. Though Greg couldn't help but feel like a disappointment to his namesake lineage with his medical discharge in the place of a full career of service, he still had the example they'd set for him. The strength they'd infused in him pretty much from birth.

His grandfather was gone, but when William Wesley had been alive, he'd been not only the rock of their family but the calmest bastion of strength in any crisis. As Randolph Wesley was now. Both were men of few words, and yet there'd never been a doubt as to who they were, what they expected and what others could expect from them. Their presence had been and was steady, dependable and loyal.

And there'd never been any doubt in Greg's mind

that he'd been expected to be the next career soldier. "Hooah" was the way his father had told him good-night every night since Greg was a baby. When he was old enough to understand, he'd taken comfort and pride from the intimate—between him and his dad only—understanding of who they were. Loyal. Committed. Always there for each other, and for others, too. Greg took on the persona willingly.

No way he was going to chicken out. Not out of life. And not out of flying. He was strong. Able to take on challenges for himself and others. He was one who gave service, not one who took it.

Weakness would not debilitate him.

He would not disappoint his father again.

But as he stood beneath the rising sun, approaching the plane, it wasn't his father he was thinking of. Wendy Alvarez was the person pushing him. It was her face he saw encouraging him. Her voice he heard in his mind.

No way he was going to let down her Pets for Vets program.

Or his own Pilots for Paws.

And no way in hell he was going to have her thinking of him as less of a man. He couldn't have her believing he was someone who'd let her down. One who was unreliable or disloyal to their cause.

Not because he hoped to build something personal with her. He didn't.

But because she was counting on him.

And because she'd respected his ability to help

himself. She'd offered assistance, both the night of the storm and the previous night, as well. And when he'd said no, she'd accepted that he'd made his choice without trying to make him feel as though he'd made the wrong one.

She'd called him to fly for her again, showing faith in him. In his abilities. Hardly the action of a woman who saw him in need of fixing.

And he was going to make damned sure that he didn't do anything to let her down. On sure feet, with no hesitation now, he strode to the door of the plane. Climbed up into the cockpit. Settling himself in the pilot's seat, he looked at the controls. Reached to start the engine.

And stared at his shaking hand.

All he could think about was getting out of his seat, out of the cockpit. Onto solid ground.

But he couldn't go anywhere. He hadn't conducted his preflight check. Or radioed a take-off. There was absolutely no reason for him to panic. And there was absolutely no denying that that was what he was doing.

He forced himself to go through the motions, to look at dials. Put himself into mental run-throughs of the purpose of and proper setting for every knob and switch, every round-windowed gauge, as though taking an exam.

Focus beat fear.

Or at least, that was the plan. He thought it might be working at first, through sheer force of will, but then his head started to feel heavy, almost drugged, and he knew he had to get out of the plane.

To breathe.

Stumbling back to his car, he didn't allow himself to think about the cockpit or of himself inside it. He shoved his thoughts away from any replay of the major failure he'd just experienced.

And turned onto the highway. Wide-open space.

But more importantly, the road to getting his head straight. To a visit that would remind him who and what he was.

And wasn't.

Because Wendy Alvarez and the prospect of her disappointment in him was weighing far too heavily on his mind. Weighing him down.

He couldn't let a woman, any woman, get to him to the point of him starting to develop deep, personal caring about her opinion or otherwise. And when he was more worried about disappointing her than his father or himself, that signaled that the caring had gone too deep.

It took him forty-five minutes to get to his destination. Another ten to get parked and inside. The private facility did everything they could to make the place seem welcoming and cheerful, but the long-term care facility still seemed to carry a certain pall, despite the manicured grounds and large windows letting in lots of light. The woman at the reception desk just smiled and waved him through. All of the staff knew him by sight. After all, he visited every Wednesday, without fail.

"Hey, bro," he greeted the man strapped upright in a wheelchair, his mouth hanging open, his head tilting awkwardly. His eyes were open, but they stared out, unfocused and unseeing. "I had some extra time today so I'm early. Figured we could watch the game together. Red Sox are favored to beat the Blue Jays today, my man."

His comrade in arms, fellow soldier, the man he'd carried out of the exploding desert hellhole, gave no sign of having heard him.

Or knowing that anyone had entered his room.

But Greg kept trying. The doctors couldn't say for sure that Duke couldn't hear. Didn't know whether or not the man understood what was said around him.

Duke breathed on his own. His body processed nourishment sent through his feeding tube and disposed of waste. He was staying alive without life support. And if you spooned chocolate pudding or ice cream into his mouth, he swallowed it.

He had daily therapy and was on very little medication, and there he sat. A man who'd been on track to make general before the rest of them. Most of the rest of the soldiers caught in that blast hadn't survived.

Greg sat through the game with Duke. Talking to him as though the man he'd known was sitting right there with him. And during commercials, he read the day's news from his phone, discussing current affairs, sharing his opinion, as he'd once done.

Greg had to do what he could to keep Duke prepared to step out into the world in the event the man was still in there and was ever able to find his way out.

A couple of times, Greg opened his mouth to tell his closest brother in arms about coming down in the storm. He ached to hear Duke tell him to get his ass back in the plane and up in the sky, but each time, he closed his mouth again without saying a word. Duke didn't need to be burdened with his woes. The man had enough of his own. And Greg's inconveniences…they completely paled in comparison to the challenges Duke faced every single day of his life.

He didn't talk about Wendy, either, for different reasons. A guy talking to a guy about a woman… made the woman something in the guy's life.

And she wasn't.

Couldn't be.

No way he was going to ask Wendy, or anyone, to be in a relationship with him. He couldn't even trust his sleeping self to keep her safe. It was humiliating that he'd had a nightmare when he'd slept on her couch, but it could have been worse. What if she'd gotten too close during his nightmare and he'd struck her? There was a reason he didn't want anyone near him while he slept, and it wasn't just a matter of keeping his private business private. It was a matter of safety, too.

Wendy was safer without him. And that was why, when she called twice, midafternoon, he didn't pick up.

The game went into extra innings, and Greg, with no great incentive to get back to thoughts of panic, lost track of time.

Until it was too late.

"Oh!" He heard the female voice at the same time he became aware that Duke's door had pushed open behind him. "Greg, you're here later than usual."

Julie—Duke's sister, his only family, a woman who stopped by to see her brother every single day on her way home from work—didn't have to sound quite so glad to see him.

"The game went over," he said, standing abruptly, pushing the chair he'd pulled up beside Duke back to its usual position in the corner of the room. "I'll go now, though."

She didn't argue or try to persuade him to stay. The two of them… It seemed to hurt both of them to be together with a comatose Duke.

Stopping by Duke's chair, he clamped the man on the shoulder, held tight for a moment. "Hooah, bro."

"Thanks for coming." Julie took the seat he'd just vacated, pulling yarn and the metal hooked needle she always used out of her bag. "I know it means a lot to him." She nodded toward her younger brother.

Greg nodded, too. Wished her a good-night, strode out of the room as though he had somewhere to be, propelled by the guilt that consumed him every single time he read the pain on Julie's face.

It should have been Greg, not Duke, who'd been so badly injured. His sisters had each other and their spouses. His parents had each other and his sisters. And Julie...she only had Duke.

But it hadn't been Greg who'd been hit worst by the blast. His leg had been injured, but his life and his mind had been spared. He owed it to Duke. To the comrades in their platoon who'd died that day. And he didn't intend to use his life to honor them by chickening out.

Or letting fear win.

He owed it to himself. And to the people still in his life. His family.

Wendy.

He wasn't open to a committed partner relationship, but he could be a friend. A damned good one.

He would fly again.

He had to fly again.

He wasn't going to let Wendy down.

No matter what.

Chapter Six

Sitting outside in a folding camp chair, her feet flat on the grass of the caged enclosure, Wendy constricted her breathing, consciously tightening her chest, refusing to relax it as she felt her heart rate speed up. She thought of being down in a mine and having the elevator that was meant to take her back up break down. Hearing a drizzle of rock fall in the distance. Eyes open but unfocused, she blocked everything but the image she was creating in her brain.

And felt a pair of paws and then full front legs crawl up and settle in her lap, followed by a big wet nose nuzzling the underside of her chin.

She grinned. He'd passed the test.

Moving her hand up to the big canine mouth so

close to her own, she held her fingers out flat, revealing the treat she had.

"Good boy, Jedidiah. Good boy!" she told the eleven-month-old German shepherd she'd had her eye on for months.

One of twenty-one dogs the Furever Paws Animal Rescue shelter had taken in after the arrest of a backyard breeder, Jedidiah was currently the only dog left, other than some moms who'd recently had pups—and Pepper, who had been one of the breeder's personal pets.

Out of the four skinny male German shepherds who'd been in the lot, Jedidiah had been the sickest, meaning he'd stayed at the rescue center even after the other three dogs had gone into the Pets for Vets program. But the dog was well on the road to recovery now, and he'd also shown signs of service-dog training right from the beginning. As though someone had started to work with him. Wendy had arranged for him to have a trainer come in as soon as Jedidiah could handle it, and the result made her heart soar.

The dog still needed extra care for his health. He'd had the hundred-and-twenty-hours' training mandated for service-dog work but hadn't yet had the thirty hours of public exposure necessary before she could match him up with one of the veterans on the Pets for Vets waiting list.

She'd had a peek at the dog's medical file and with all of the X-rays and infusions and medications, Jedidiah had already run up a bill in the thousands. He couldn't be adopted until he had a clean bill of health. And the trainer didn't want to introduce him to public exposure until then, either.

Assuming Jedidiah continued to respond well to treatment and got healthy.

Giving the dog a hug, petting him, finding her calm by doing so, she made up her mind to think positively—to feel confident that Jedidiah would get well. That the smart, eager-to-please, mistreated dog would live a long, happy life with someone who loved him.

When her phone rang, Jedidiah stepped down from her lap and wandered off to explore the enclosed grassy area behind the shelter while she pulled her phone out of her pocket and checked the screen.

Greg.

She'd left a voice mail. Hadn't liked that he hadn't returned her call. For various reasons, probably, but the most prominent one was that not hearing from him meant he could be in trouble.

Perversely, now that his call indicated he was alive, she didn't want to pick up. Didn't want him to matter so much that he'd been on her mind all afternoon, that she'd been worried about him. But then again, she didn't want him to matter so much that she dodged his calls, either.

"Hello?" Jedidiah came back as she answered, probably sensing the tension in her tone. Or her body language. The dog didn't immediately embark on providing deep pressure therapy as he had moments ago, and she counted that as a win.

She might be tense, but she wasn't exhibiting the signs of panic he'd been trained to respond to.

"I've been with a friend all afternoon, just now got free," Greg said, sounding a lot more fine than she'd been picturing him.

Note to self to take a step back. Maybe several.

"What's up?" he asked when she got too caught up in talking to herself to respond to him.

"I had an emergency run, wanted to offer it to Pilots for Paws and you're my contact, but I ended up placing it with another pilot."

"Wow. I'm sorry."

"Not a big deal," she quickly told him, standing to walk the yard with the dog who was staying close. "After this morning...I wasn't really wanting to force you to ask one of your other pilots to go up for you."

Except that she had been. She'd thought the emergency run coming in as it had was a sign—a way to get Greg back in the game even if he wasn't actually up in the sky yet. Thinking of others, doing for others, having something outside of oneself upon which to focus were all ways to help stave off panic.

She knew. Had learned everything she possibly could, more than she'd ever probably use, in her desperate need to help Michael.

And it hadn't helped.

He hadn't wanted her help. Or hadn't been willing to admit that he'd needed it. He hadn't thought she *could* help.

Was she ever going to learn?

He shouldn't have called her back. Not that late in the day. It wasn't like he'd be up for a night flight, and the only reason for them to converse was to arrange a dog transfer.

And yet, standing there in his hangar—he'd driven straight there from Duke's facility—he'd pulled out his phone and had called her back.

Like bringing her to the scene of his crime, his weakness, would somehow make it better.

Then she'd said she hadn't felt good about asking him to call another pilot when he couldn't go up himself?

What the hell? If she was going to start feeling sorry for him…making concessions as though he wasn't whole and able…

Hearing the lack of complete lucidity in his thoughts, he took a deep breath. As she'd said, he was her contact with Pilots for Paws, only one of the sources she used for pilots. He'd called other pilots on the Pilots for Paws roster several times. And if she hadn't needed them, why call them?

Because she always called him first. And would have asked him to arrange for a pilot, even knowing that he was struggling himself, if he'd picked up the phone.

Angry with himself, maybe with her, angry that

life left people like Duke injured, angry that his heart had started to pound the second he'd climbed into the cockpit that morning, angry that Wendy Alvarez sounded distant, like she was giving up on him, he blurted, "The friend I was with for most of the day… we've known each other a long time." Since boot camp—bonding first and foremost because they'd both been from North Carolina. They'd been of like mind, he and Duke—lifers who were prepared to sacrifice everything to serve and protect.

"It's fine, Greg. You don't owe me an explanation. You don't owe me anything. With all the hours of volunteer work you've done for Pets for Vets over the years, if anything I'm in your debt. Truly, we're all good."

"Duke's living in an institution," he said then, leaning his butt on the front wheel base of the plane—keeping the aircraft at his back. And touching it, too.

How could something he loved be the cause of so much stress?

"He sits in a chair, seemingly unresponsive, day after day, week after week, year after year."

And every day, Julie had stopped by after work to visit with him. A lawyer, Duke had said that she'd always been more dedicated to her work than she'd been to dating, which was why there was no romantic partner in her life. He'd mentioned how she had joked about planning to be the fun aunt to Duke's kids rather than having any of her own. And Greg knew she still worked as many hours in a day as she could squeeze in, oftentimes bringing work into Duke's room with her.

Maybe she went out with friends, too. Maybe she dated these days. It wasn't like she spent the entire night in her brother's room.

But it was pretty much certain that she was never going to be a favorite aunt to Duke's kids.

Wendy hadn't responded, leaving silence between them.

She hadn't hung up, either, this woman who seemed to spend as much or more time volunteering in the Pets for Vets program as Julie spent sitting in Duke's room.

"He was on his second tour of duty in Afghanistan. Rank, second lieutenant. Conducting routine reconnaissance. The attack came out of nowhere. Shots coming down from a mountain peak. He never knew what hit him."

"I'm so sorry."

Her tone…it held understanding, not pity. Because of all of her work with vets?

He started to tell her that he'd been there, too. But then, most likely the pity would finally come. She'd see more into his challenges than what was there—after all, she hadn't expected him to be able to fly for her. She'd called but wasn't counting on him as she'd always done. He was already appearing less dependable.

No way he was going to be that guy. Afghanistan

had already taken far too much from him. It wasn't taking his identity as someone who could help, someone who could be counted on.

"I've gone to see him every Wednesday since he came home." Some mornings, some afternoons, a few times late at night after Julie had left, arranging visits around his schedule. Maybe Duke knew he came, maybe not. But if Duke was aware of it in any way, he'd be relying on Greg to be there.

"I'm guessing that on some level he knows."

It was like she'd read his mind. Or his hopes. What was it with the woman, seeming to know him better than was logical? Knowing more about his private struggle than he was giving her?

He didn't want that, either.

"Have you been up in the plane at all today?"

A valid question, considering the circumstances. He should have gone up that morning. After the scare, he should have climbed down out of the cockpit, done his preflight check as he would normally have done, logged in the flight and headed up. Even if just for a few minutes.

Instead, he'd hung up from her and run to Duke.

"It was my day to see Duke." The excuse was lame, and he was sure she knew it. He'd flown for Wendy on Wednesdays before and had gone to see Duke either before or afterward.

"A dog could help, Greg." Her tone came softly, but with the firmness he'd grown to expect from her. She told things like they were.

One of the first things he'd liked about her.

"I don't need a dog."

He needed to quit giving in to his fears and fly. He was a pilot, damn it.

Not a broken man.

Luckily Wendy had a busy day at the office on Thursday, with back-to-back appointments most of the morning. The work offered a needed distraction from the hurt and frustration that had been brewing since she'd hung up from Greg the evening before.

Over the drive home from the shelter Wednesday, during dinner and throughout the miserable fail of an attempt to get through the pile of work she'd brought with her, the frustration had simmered, growing hotter, until it had bubbled up into something she had to face.

And it gave her something to focus on other than the hurt—the tears that had sprung so shockingly to her eyes when Greg had rejected her offer to help him.

Lord knew, her skin was tougher than that. All the vets she'd helped over the years…denial of any need for help was a common part of the process. There was no reason for her to take it so personally.

Yet, she had.

She was.

Because he was shutting her out.

Like Michael had.

And her father continued to do.

Greg wasn't her family. But he was important to her.

What was it with the men in her life? Why did they seem to think that it was okay to turn away from her as though she had nothing to offer?

To banish her?

Well, it wasn't going to happen again. She wasn't just going to turn her back while Greg hid his need from himself, as though admitting that he could use some help made him less of a man. What hiding did was let the insidious problem grow until his personhood became so diminished that he lost sight of its value.

When that happened, there was too much of a risk of him deciding to just end his life. The way Michael had. The way their mother had, indirectly, via alcohol in the years after Michael's suicide.

Shaking as she walked to the corner pub for some dinner and a beer—and for some time not alone— she shut her mind down to Michael and that first devastating loss, to the horrifying memories of coming home from school to find her yard ablaze with swirling lights, the driveway and street filled with emergency vehicles...

She pushed all of that aside and thought about what sounded good to eat.

Looked for her usual corner table on the outdoor patio—the one set under a sourwood tree that provided shade to the rest of the patio—and gratefully took a sip of the beer that followed her to her seat.

Along with smiles and a bit of catching up with the waitress who'd delivered it.

It was nice to be known. To have one's wants anticipated without having to speak them.

It was nice to be appreciated.

And maybe sometimes, it was necessary to fight.

She'd been a kid when Michael had been struggling, when her mother had drunk herself to death, and her dad?

She'd been so afraid of losing him, too, that she'd put up with his distance, never making an issue of it.

Never letting him know how much it hurt.

Never fighting for more time with him.

Even as she sat there thinking about it all, she didn't know how to bridge that gap with her father.

But she wasn't going to let Greg Martin push her away.

And just like that, as though ideas had been stirring in her subconscious over the past twenty-four hours, the answer came to her. Without analyzing or even real thought, she pulled her phone out of her back pocket and dialed.

He picked up on the first ring.

Smart man.

"I have a favor to ask," she said before he'd even finished his *Hello*. "Not a flight. Something else."

"Sure. What's up?"

"I've been working with a dog at the Furever Paws Animal Rescue here in Spring Forest, an eleven-month-old German shepherd. He's had service-dog training and from the very beginning has shown more promise than any dog I've ever worked with, but he's got some continuing health issues that concern me." She barely paused for air. Didn't want him interrupting her while she was on a roll. Didn't want time to think of all the reasons her plan wouldn't work. "He needs to be fostered, to have more individualized home care, to help him recover more quickly and also to get him ready to serve—"

"If you're going to ask me to take in a foster dog, Wendy, stop right there. You think I'm that gullible? You can't get me to agree to a dog's help, so you're going to foist one on me by framing it as a favor?"

Pretty much. Yeah. "I wasn't going to ask you to take him, Greg," she almost bit out, frustration growing even stronger. How many times was the guy going to reject her?

"He needs to stay in Spring Forest," she continued with forced calm, while her knee bobbed faster than a drum could beat. "For veterinary care," she added, so he'd know she wasn't making it up. "He's on a routine after transfusions, with medications and things." She wasn't going to get into all that.

"An eleven-month-old dog had to have transfusions?" His tone, the surprised concern, gave her hope.

"Among other things, yes. I spoke with Bethany yesterday, she's the center's manager, and Jedidiah's bills are astronomical. They're hoping to have a fundraiser soon to take care of the mounting costs for Jedidiah and the other animals that were rescued at the same time as him, and adoptions of other animals are happening very quickly, which brings in a little money, but they can't continue to pay for Jedidiah's training, and the girl they hired to do it can't afford to work for free..."

He asked what had happened to Jedidiah to begin with. She told him about the earlier arrest of the backyard breeder, and then she went straight to the point.

"I've been working with Jedidiah, and I want to foster him, but there are days that I have to spend in my office, and I won't have time to give him the training and attention he needs. I can arrange my office time so that it's specific days a week, but there are certain clients I meet with in person and... Anyway, I was wondering, since you've been so eager to volunteer and you know the program..." she pulled out all the stops, shamelessly "... I was hoping you'd be willing to help out at my place, to work with Jedidiah at least part of the time I can't be there—though, I have to say, it would be best if you could cover all the days that I work so he has consistency with his training. The sessions have to happen at intervals throughout the day. And he needs his medication at the same time every day, as well."

She paused for air and took heart when Greg didn't immediately jump into the pause with more rejection.

"Hearing you talk yesterday about Duke, I realized that you have an understanding of these vets that's personal, something you can't teach a person, and you could be a big help in testing Jedidiah's level of training."

She paused again. To silence.

"It would only be until Jedidiah's ready to go to work," she told him. "Could even just be a matter of weeks, if home care is as beneficial to speeding up his recovery as I think it will be."

"You've known the dog a while?"

"Several months."

"And he really shows remarkable promise?"

"More than I've ever seen. He's aware, astute. He tunes in to people in a natural way." All true.

"Okay. Yeah. You'll need to leave me with specific instructions—and I do mean specific, if there's timing of medication involved, since I'll need to be on top of that."

Okay? Yeah?

Seriously?

He was going to do it?

"Fine," she said, after a sip of beer meant to drown the joy coursing through her. "I'll call Bethany at the animal rescue first thing in the morning, finalize arrangements and get back to you."

She needed to order dinner.

And get Bethany on the phone. Why wait until morning?

There were other things, too, like...getting a dog dish? And a bed?

"I'm glad you called." Greg's words shocked all thought out of her brain.

"Yeah, well, you know me, always begging for what I need for my dogs and vets…" She thanked him and hung up before she said something truly stupid. But mentally, she was doing a little dance of glee as she ordered a beef and cheese–laden enchilada for dinner, her future artery health be damned. Tonight, she was celebrating.

Chapter Seven

After a long day of board meetings for one of the nonprofits he managed—a national organization set up to match private pilots with service organizations, such as the Pilots for Paws program—Greg had stopped by his favorite gourmet sub shop to pick up dinner and had driven straight to the airstrip.

He'd been sitting in his cockpit, enjoying the sandwich and scrolling on his phone, when Wendy had called. Eating something he particularly favored while looking over something pleasantly engrossing had been his plan to combat the panic that was threatening to ground him.

He'd been sitting there with no preflight check and no logged flight, so no pressure to take her up.

All purposeful steps in his self-imposed recovery program.

He hadn't thought to include a phone call in his regime, but as he hung up from speaking with Wendy, he definitely wasn't experiencing any panic regarding the plane or the sky. He wasn't even thinking about them.

His chest was tight due to an entirely different stimulus—namely, the prospect of spending many hours, regularly, in her home.

With the way she'd framed it, agreeing had been a no-brainer. She'd mentioned Duke and men like him benefiting. Greg had to do it.

But he didn't have to be feeling a lift in his mood over it.

He didn't have to be curious to be in her home again—to spend periods of time there.

Didn't have to be okay with seeing her again soon—and often.

Where were his defenses when he needed them?

Busy fighting off fake demons, that was where. He'd been told, many times, that the only thing he had to fear was fear itself...meaning that flying, the storm, a near crash weren't keeping him from his first love.

Fear was doing that.

Not in that moment. He was good, sitting there with his phone and his picnic in the cockpit. Of course, he knew he wasn't going to try to take the plane up.

And his emotions were otherwise engaged. Lingering in a small home on the outskirts of Spring Forest, rather than in a storm. His mind, rather than replaying a near crash, was conjuring up images of low lights and soft conversation with a friend who was suddenly becoming a closer friend.

But the landing, if he played out his mental scenario with Wendy, wouldn't be any better than coming down in that deserted drive-in had been. And could be a whole lot worse.

If he gave in to his urges to spend more time with Wendy, if he allowed himself to explore any possibilities...his own heart, his own life, wouldn't be the only potential victim. When things couldn't come to a natural conclusion, when he couldn't offer Wendy any more than daytime and evening companionship, there'd be a crash. And there was no way he could take a chance on more, on sharing a life with her that included sleeping. He would not put her in that danger. Which meant he couldn't let Wendy fall for him. Even a little bit.

Still, while the day before, just being in the cockpit had brought on panic, there he was in his seat in front of the controls, calmly eating a sandwich.

Which meant, by his calculation, he had a win! He'd successfully completed the first step of his program. Spending time in the cockpit without a panic attack. The next one, doing a preflight check without logging a flight, would happen...momentarily.

As soon as he'd finished his dinner. And done some phone research on service dogs.

And maybe, in the morning, he'd log a flight. Maybe even start the plane. Taxi in her.

If all went well, he'd be flying again by the end of the weekend...

And would be able to be of piloting service to Wendy again.

While he couldn't be her lover, he'd be back to being the friend who was there for her whenever she needed him. For flying. And now for the dog, as well.

Hell, if all went well, he might just try to let himself need her friendship, too.

Wendy lived for pets. For the veterans that she served with her whole heart. For the townspeople who meant so much to her. She didn't bring any of them into her home.

And there she was, Friday noon, with an eleven-month-old German shepherd staring at her from the passenger seat of her SUV, on his way to move in with her.

"I have to warn you, buddy, this is just temporary. I'm not your forever home. I'm in and out all the time, which is why I don't adopt anyone. But I've made arrangements for you, don't worry..."

Jedidiah could leave the worrying up to her.

She'd called Greg that morning, as soon as she'd confirmed through Bethany that the veterinarian had signed off on releasing Jedidiah to home care and she was welcome to come get him.

Greg hadn't picked up.

Or called back.

He was a busy man, she got that. And she had a case of the guilts over trying to get Jedidiah and Greg together—for both their sakes, not just the dog's, as she'd claimed.

Maybe it was wrong of her, not being completely honest with Greg, but...she'd rather have a dishonesty mark on her integrity than have another man die because she hadn't been able to do enough.

It wasn't like she was forcing Greg to help her out. Or forcing him to take Jedidiah. She was just placing the two of them in proximity and then waiting to let nature take its course.

And hoping.

And if she was getting in too deep?

If she got hurt in the process?

She could handle it. Of that she was certain. She knew how to find her own happiness.

Jedidiah nudged her elbow—looking for reassurance? He hadn't left the shelter since he'd been rescued, receiving all veterinary care in-house.

Reaching over to scratch behind the dog's ear, she said, "It's going to be good for you, Jedidiah, or I'll take you right back." The words were a promise. "You know me. You know you can trust me," she continued. If he didn't get the words, he'd get the tone of voice. "You're going to meet Greg this afternoon, and he could be your forever love. Your forever family. I'm not promising that part, but I want you to know that that's the plan for you. Forever love with a person you adore. And Greg...he's one of the most decent human beings I've ever met."

The words flew out of her and stopped the path of her thoughts the second she heard them out loud.

Instead of thinking about the dog's future, she was thinking about the man she'd be introducing Jedidiah to. Greg had become a friend over the years. Someone who engaged in harmless flirting with her. Someone she could always count on. But there was more to what she felt for him than what she usually acknowledged.

Greg really was one of the most decent human beings she'd ever met. The knowledge had grown on her over time without her even being aware... and yet, there it was.

And that explained why she was so personally invested in trying to help him. It was because he was such a good guy. Because he deserved the help. With all that he'd done for her over the years, he'd earned her respect.

It was not because of any personal feelings she had for him. No, surely not.

She reminded herself of that a couple of hours later when her home was once again consumed by Greg's broad shoulders stretching the boundaries of his white shirt as he immediately squatted down in those perfect-fitting black shorts to put himself on eye level with Jedidiah for their first introduction.

She was only fulfilling a bargain, not falling for the guy.

"Hey, Jedi." His soft male tones sent tingles through her. *Jedi.*

He had given the dog a nickname. That meant something.

"Jedi?" she said aloud, because she had to keep herself firmly on track. "Like in *Star Wars*?"

"Exactly. He's one of the good guys," Greg said, half over his shoulder without taking his eyes off the dog. "Jedis are warriors," he told the dog. "They save the world and fight bad things, but only with peace, never violence. And that's you, isn't it?"

Tears sprang to her eyes.

Wendy excused herself to use the restroom.

And was relieved when it appeared that neither of the male entities invading her space seemed to notice.

"You ever have pets growing up?" Wendy's question, coming in the middle of her tutoring session Friday evening, with him focused on learning Jedi's schedule and specific needs, had him answering without filtering.

"No. My sister was allergic."

"You have a sister?"

"Two of them."

"Younger or older?"

"One of each," he said, looking over the sheets she'd handed him. One had a monthly calendar through July, with scheduled times written in, asterisks by the days that were flexible if he needed a particular day off, and stars by the days she could work from home if she had to, with the caveat that those starred days could change at any time.

The other sheets stapled together were Jedi's training instructions.

He was keeping his mind on the things that he'd chosen to become involved with and off the way Wendy's V-neck tank top dipped, offering a discreet peek at her cleavage. The way her fingers trailed lightly, almost unconsciously, over Jedi's head and neck, back and forth, back and forth. The way he could almost feel those fingers on his skin...

"What about your parents?" she asked.

"What about them?"

"Are they close by?"

"They retired to Arizona." And why was he the one on the witness stand? "What about you? Did you have pets as a kid?"

"For a while."

Didn't tell him much. Probably for the best.

"We had a dog and a cat," she elaborated. "Then just a cat."

He nodded, an image flashing across his brain of what she might have looked like as a kid. "Did you wear your hair in a braid then, too?"

"Always. My mom's choice to begin with, but then mine."

"Is she close by?" Jedi's gaze turned to him as he spoke.

Was that his way of reminding Greg that the dog was supposed to be the topic of conversation?

It would be good to know if family members could be stopping by while he was in Wendy's home, he silently answered the nosy shepherd. Good to know whether she'd mentioned him to them—if they knew he'd be there, and why.

"She died when I was sixteen," she told him.

The words delivered a bit of a gut punch. A girl losing her mom at sixteen… That couldn't have been easy. "What about your dad?"

"He and my stepmom live in Raleigh, but they're on a six-month cruise around the world right now."

Interesting. The mom dies. The dad is distant…

Told him more about Wendy in a minute than he'd learned in all the years he'd known her.

Or explained some of the things her actions had told him. Her independence, for one.

And nothing else he needed to know. They'd been through his complete training session. Time for him to go.

"I'll call him Jedidiah if you feel that I should," he said, mentioning the small thing that had been on his mind since she'd abruptly left the room after he'd nicknamed the dog. "The whole movie franchise, including the Jedis, had me hooked as a kid…"

"Well, with your love of flying, it makes sense."

Right. Felt kind of...comfortable...her knowing him that well.

Her grin hit him in the stomach. In a sinfully delicious way. "*Jedi*'s fine," she said, drawing the dog's gaze up to her, his nose nudging her thigh, as he heard his name.

"See, he knows it already," he told her, like he could somehow take credit for that.

She nodded, her gaze colliding head-on with Greg's, when they both looked up from the dog at the same time. Like cars with locked bumpers, they stood there, blue eyes hooked to green, as though neither of them knew how to get them apart.

A prod at his thigh pulled Greg's attention a bit, but it wasn't until Wendy stepped back and he glanced down to see the dog that had insinuated himself between them that he finally escaped the woman's allure.

Saved by the dog.

And Greg wondered, as he said good-night, if he was there to teach Jedi or if the dog was there to teach him.

Either way, lesson learned.

He had to make certain that, over the next weeks of helping train a service dog, he kept his distance from Jedi's foster caregiver.

Chapter Eight

What was that?

In bed, eyes still closed, Wendy came slowly to consciousness, aware that she'd heard something. It took a moment before she remembered that she had another living being in the house.

Jedi must be awake.

Eyes popping open, she focused on the spot beside the bed where the dog had been lying when she'd awoken at some point during the night. Their third night together.

She hadn't slept through any of the three, still adjusting to having breathing in the house other than her own.

The spot on the floor was empty. And when she

felt a shove against her calf as the bed dipped, she knew why. Jedi had been on the bed with her.

"Jedi?" She heard the voice…had no time to comprehend…

The dog barked and then jumped down, just as Greg came down the hall toward her.

Grabbing the covers up to her neck as she saw him, she knew she hadn't acted in time. He'd seen her.

And seen the way the tank top she was wearing had got twisted up in her sleep to show way more than she ever would have intended. Her body grew a little warm inside her panties.

She heard his muttered "Oh, God…" too, as he turned his back, heading in the opposite direction.

"Oh, God," she reiterated right back at him.

And then, "Traitor," she muttered under her breath when the dog she'd spent the weekend welcoming into her home trotted down the hall after her intruder.

What the hell? Monday's schedule clearly stated that Jedi's first session started at ten. A glance at the clock on her bedside table showed that it was only eight. She dressed quickly, pulling on a bra, a T-shirt and some shorts—a favorite pair of old cut-off sweatpants that hung to her knees.

Not bothering with a toothbrush, not caring that little hairs stuck out like bristles from her night-tousled braid, she traipsed down the hall.

For coffee.

To find out why in the hell Greg Martin was at her house two hours early.

To see if he'd already run out on them the morning of his first official day as Jedi's helpmate.

But no, she already knew that he hadn't run. She'd have heard the door if he had. And anyway, Greg wasn't a runner. So she wasn't surprised to find him standing at the living-room window, back straight, hands in the pockets of his jeans, facing the street. The stance might have been less…haunting…if the curtain had been open.

The blame she'd been about to heap upon him—mostly propelled by the heightened emotion swarming through her—froze on her lips.

"What's wrong?" Had he had another accident with the plane? Or tried to go up and panicked again? Had he come to her for help?

"Your schedule clearly states that you started work at eight this morning," he stated, shooting an arm behind him to show her a piece of paper with fold creases.

Right. She'd put her work times down just for full disclosure. So he'd know how long Jedi had been alone when he arrived. So he'd know whether she'd be around, in case he was going to be late.

He hadn't come to her—or Jedi—because he needed them. He'd merely come to work early, assuming she'd already be up, dressed and gone.

"I had a client who received an IRS audit notice on Saturday. Other than tending to Jedi, I've been working pretty much nonstop ever since, so I decided to go in a little late this morning."

Whether it was the shaky tone in her voice, or her acknowledgment that she hadn't done what she'd written she'd be doing, or something else entirely of which she was unaware…Greg finally turned around to face her.

"I'm sorry." For pointing out her mistake? Invading her home when she was asleep? Seeing way more than expected of her breasts?

"Me, too."

"He was sleeping on your bed." What? Who?

Greg's hand reached for Jedi, who'd been standing there nudging him.

Right. The dog.

"He's been kennel-sleeping his whole life. Once he's put into service, he'll be on call night and day with his owner—alert to the onset of migraine symptoms, for instance—so he can wake his owner in time to take a pill before the headache gets severe." She was rambling, but she didn't know how to stop. "Part of training him includes keeping him close enough, even when he's sleeping, or I am."

Jedi's nudges against Greg were growing more insistent.

"I have frozen symptomatic saliva from a migraine patient," she carried on. "We've been using it to train Jedi." If he went into service with a PTSD veteran who suffered from migraines, he'd be introduced to the scent of his new person's saliva during a headache so he'd know how to respond.

"As you said on Friday," he calmly pointed out.

"I'll introduce it during the night at some point..."

He looked so...hot...standing there with his long-ish hair adding more sexy to his rugged, bearded look.

He looked so...showered.

While she stood there definitely at her worst.

Jedi nudged again.

"He's probably hungry," she said then, before leaving the two males to fend for themselves in her home. She walked back to her room, shut the door and fell back against it.

What in the hell had she done to herself?

Greg texted Wendy before using his key at her house from that first day on. And didn't even so much as look down the hall toward her bedroom.

He'd been a little het up on Monday morning, had made the mistake of heading to Spring Forest early, particularly eager to be of service, to be needed in person, having just come from the airstrip where, for the third morning in a row, he'd taxied his plane.

And where, for the second morning in a row he'd logged a flight and then hadn't taken off.

His personal program stipulated no panic pre-flight before taking off.

He'd made it out to the runway Monday morning. And again Tuesday.

Still hadn't lifted off.

But a curious thing had happened both times. Monday morning, when he'd gone down the hall in Wendy's home, seeking Jedi, already uptight from his failure to lift off, his tension level had skyrocketed after seeing Wendy barely dressed in her bed. He'd known she had breasts, of course, but having actually seen them…having that memory seemingly on instant replay in his head…most definitely not a good thing.

Knowing that he'd made her supremely uncomfortable added another decibel to his tension level.

He'd stood there in her living room, needing to get out of there and back to his own life, his breath getting short, and Jedi had nudged him. Not once but again and again, until Greg had paid attention to him and pet his head.

Wendy had mentioned that the dog was probably hungry, but when Greg had gone to feed him, Jedi hadn't eaten a bite. Instead, he'd nudged Greg, who, not knowing what else he could do to help the young dog, had sat on the floor and played with him.

Which had distracted him.

And by the time Wendy had come out, he'd had himself back under control—and Jedi had stopped nudging him.

On Tuesday, when he'd come into the house alone, after Wendy went to work, as scheduled, he'd intended to get to work with Jedi right away. And yet, it had been a struggle to concentrate since he had been on the verge of panic every time he thought about his flight failures.

And Jedi had been there. Nudging his hand.

While Greg didn't need a service dog for himself, Jedi's attention and his ability to sense tension in Greg had shown him firsthand Jedi's remarkable talent. He'd be a great gift for some other vet. And that started him thinking a whole lot more about Wendy's Pet for Vets program.

Thinking about it beyond delivering dogs.

He gave himself a break from the airfield on Wednesday. He'd made an early-morning breakfast visit to Duke, had a quarterly virtual meeting with the office manager of a nonprofit young pilots' organization and then headed to Spring Forest. Wendy was still involved with a charter-school audit, which had her putting in crazy hours. That meant that, other than Jedi's scheduled care, the dog had been spending a lot of time having to entertain himself.

She was at the office from midmorning on Wednesday and had a late afternoon meeting at the school with the auditor, who needed to see that government funds were being properly allocated. Wendy hadn't told him many details, but from her tone, it was clear she expected the meeting to be grueling.

And he'd decided, to help her out, he'd have dinner ready for her when she got home. She could eat it, or not, as she chose, but at least she'd have the option. By his own account, he'd perfected chili over the years, and by trial and taste had found the best boxed corn bread recipe to go with it. In between sessions with Jedi, he got to work preparing both.

"I know this seems a bit sappy," he told the German shepherd, who sat watching him with soulful brown eyes as he chopped. "But I have a favor to ask."

That didn't come out right. He'd be making dinner regardless of the favor...

And that wasn't right, either, he interrupted his own thought. They'd arranged for him to be there to look after Jedidiah. Looking after Wendy had never been part of the agreement. Certainly making dinner wasn't part of the training he was on-site to provide to the dog.

But Wendy was a friend. Had been for years.

Just because he'd seen her nearly bare body, salivated over it in his dreams the past couple of nights, didn't change the reality of their situation.

With the cooking-dinner-for-a-friend situation worked out in his brain mostly to his satisfaction, he stirred the ground beef that was browning—in somewhat large chunks because he'd determined they made for better chili—and turned back to the dog.

"You need time among people, bro," he started in as he chopped an onion. "Not my call. Regulations say so. And I have an idea..."

Better not to mention it to Jedi yet, though, not until he had Wendy's approval.

She was, after all, the boss around there.

He and Jedi...they were just two cogs in her wheel. Equal cogs.

Friends to her, each in their own way.

Except that, when she came home tired and hungry that night and tilted her nose up and sniffed the air filled with the scent of chili, her gaze searching—probably for him, since he had texted to let her know he was waiting around with a favor to ask—when her gaze met his and he saw the emotion welling there... for that second, he didn't feel like just a friend.

Dropping the leather satchel she used for carrying her laptop and paper files, Wendy almost tripped over the strap in her haste to get to Jedi. To pet the dog and say hello to him. To cover up any hint of the surge of turmoil raging through her at the sight of the gorgeous helper standing in her kitchen looking all domesticated.

He wasn't wearing an apron or holding a spoon. Didn't appear any different than he had any other time she'd seen him. But with the pot of chili on the stove, the aroma in the air...the man just there, in her home, a fellow human being greeting her after a long day at work...

The sensory stimulus was a bit...overwhelming.

She could be forgiven for wanting to walk straight over and give him a hug. To lift her lips to his.

Instead, she said, "Hey, Jedi, did you have a good day?"

Taking the dog's wagging tail as an affirmative,

she then reached immediately for the stack of bowls in her cupboard. Ceramic, colorful, just as her mama's had been. She snagged two.

"I'm not eating." She didn't turn around when Greg made the pronouncement. Didn't want to give him any chance to see that his response had disappointed her.

"Why not?"

"I made it for you."

Well, that just made no sense. There was enough chili in the pot to serve eight people. At least. "It's after seven o'clock. What are you going to do for dinner?"

"Stop on the way home. There's a barbecue place right on my route."

"That's stupid." She wasn't usually so harsh, but at the moment she was peeved. The words slipped out.

"Excuse me?"

"You make dinner but won't eat it with me?" Her gaze held fire when she looked at him, and if he read the challenge there, then good. It wasn't like she was trying to hide it.

He had the grace to look a little sheepish. "I knew you'd be tired and wanted you to be able to come home and just relax, not have to be worrying about having to entertain…"

Bringing both bowls to the counter by the stove, she grabbed a ladle and started dishing out the mouthwatering meal that had been a boring staple in her home growing up. "Why don't you stop thinking for me?" she said, still sounding a bit peevish, and then added, "Besides, who said I was going to entertain? I might not even speak again. My mama taught me that it's impolite to talk with your mouth full."

Smart man that he was, he didn't respond. Instead, he reached for the door of the toaster oven, pulling out warmed corn bread.

What was the guy trying to do to her?

"I have a favor to ask," he said about two bites into the meal.

And then it all made sense, him cooking for her, staying to eat. It wasn't like he was taking them to a new level. It was because he needed something. She'd known that. He'd texted about a favor. She started to relax. "Shoot."

"I want to take Jedi with me to see Duke next week."

He considered that a favor?

More like a godsend! Even more so than the most delicious chili she'd ever had.

"He needs to start logging public hours," Greg continued, "and I'd like to see what happens. I'm guessing nothing, at least not with Duke, but some of the other guys there..."

"Are they all veterans?"

"On his wing, yes. It's a private facility, but they get some government assistance for their work with vets. They usually don't take patients onto the wing who are so unresponsive, but my old man put in a word about Duke's service, his medal..."

His old man. Who lived in Arizona?

"Your father has pull with the military?" Normally she wouldn't have asked such a question, but ordinarily Greg didn't speak enough words strung together to fill a paragraph.

Ordinarily, they didn't eat together. As in, never before now.

"He's a retired brigadier general."

Okay. She was impressed. "Wow."

He shrugged, dunked corn bread into his chili and consumed the whole thing in one bite.

"Anyone else in your family serve?" she asked, mostly just to give herself some time to catch up with everything. Him cooking for her. Them sitting at her dining-room table together. Him actually opening up for a second. She had this sense of urgency, a need to squeeze out as much as she could before he clammed up again.

"My grandfather."

"Don't tell me. He was a general, too?"

"Full colonel."

"And yet you got out?" His Pilot of Paws bio said that he'd been in the army. He wasn't anymore.

He shrugged. "My life went in a different direction."

Interesting.

"How long were you in?"

"A few years."

"Private rank?" She spent her life helping people who had been in service. She made it a point to understand their world. As though, somehow, she could turn back the clock and understand Michael.

"Second lieutenant." So he'd been an officer, not an enlisted man. That made sense, actually, if he came from a family of career soldiers.

She was still processing that when he added, almost defensively, "My grandfather died, leaving me a large inheritance. Enough that I can live off the investment returns for the rest of my life."

So, he chose a career of managing his money over service. Most would. And yet…

"These nonprofits you volunteer with…they wouldn't happen to be yours, would they?" No way the Greg Martin she knew would take a cushy, rich life over serving.

But she could believe he'd get out of the army if he saw an opportunity to serve in a bigger way.

"Some of them are."

He wasn't just a volunteer. Impressive.

And a bit intimidating, too.

Bunny and Birdie had told her that he lived in a gorgeous home, but they hadn't mentioned that he was rich and came from an obviously powerful family.

Of course, the women wouldn't put a whole lot of stock in such things. Not to gossip about it with a volunteer who spent time at their shelter. After all, they'd come from money, too, but they were never the sort to put on airs over it.

And there she was, little renting-a-small-house-bookkeeping-accountant-Wendy, thinking Greg Martin needed anything that she could offer. How silly of her.

But no sooner had she had that thought than she remembered Greg's anxiety over flying. Money didn't fix what ailed Greg. And the things he'd just told her, the powerful men who'd bred him… it wouldn't be easy for him to admit to himself, let alone anyone else, that he might need some help.

Michael had been the same: adamant, so sure he knew what was right, certain that he knew best for himself.

Her goal where Greg was concerned, her determination, her reasons for both hadn't changed.

So neither had their reasons for being together.

"I'm fine with you taking Jedi to see Duke," she said then, in between spoonfuls of chili. "If you wouldn't mind, I'd actually like to tag along. To see how he does. Jedi, that is…" Yep, she was back on task.

Right up until Greg smiled at her, thanked her and she got all warm and fuzzy inside again.

Chapter Nine

Wendy worked from home all day on Thursday, so once again, Greg took himself to the airstrip. He did his preflight check. He radioed a short flight, taxied, and…off he went. Down the runway, gaining speed and up in the air. Filled with elation, he gave a big whoop, hit a small pocket of turbulence and hit instant panic. He had to get down.

It was all he could think about, landing the plane. On his headset, he stated coordinates, radioed a landing. Focused on listening for responses. He circled, sweating, hearing an ID he knew well, Beechcraft 1472, an older pilot he'd known for years, stating his location a mile behind Greg, coming in for landing. He had to get down to make room for Nate, Beechcraft 1472. And swiftly and smoothly came in for a perfect landing.

Short of breath, he taxied to just outside his hangar, brought the plane to a stop and gasped for air.

As he sucked in breaths, he told himself that the good news was he still knew how to fly and to do it well. He'd known to focus only on the job at hand, not to think about the sweating, the pounding of his heart, the shortness of breath.

Bad news...well, he wasn't going to look for that. Not going to dwell on it.

He'd done what he'd set his mind to doing: he'd flown safely.

And kept that in mind as Nate Bailey, still with headset in hand, came walking into his hangar five minutes later.

"You got a problem with her?" the older man asked, nodding toward Greg's plane. "I heard you radio take-off five minutes before landing. Something go wrong with the work Randy did?"

Warren knew about the emergency landing, the damage to Greg's plane. He'd been around when Randy Mitchell had been working to repair the damage.

He absolutely did not know about Greg's personal struggles. Which were quickly becoming moot, anyway.

"She's fine," he said, also nodding toward his plane. "Just wanted to take her up quickly as a check before putting her back in service for Pets for Vets."

Truth. If by "her" he meant himself.

He didn't mention the brief flight to Wendy when she came for lunch on Friday to take Jedi out in public, the first of three outings they'd planned after committing to taking the dog to see Duke the following Wednesday.

Jedi had to log in thirty public hours before he could be put into service, and Wendy, after consulting with Jedi's former paid trainer at Furever Paws, had announced that the dog needed time out among people before they took him to visit a facility filled with possibly anxious patients.

Wendy would serve as Jedi's handler. Greg was a stand-in for Jedi's eventual owner. The dog had to be trained, among other things, to pay attention only to Greg's biological status, not to any of the other people who might or might not be exuding panic or migraine-like symptoms around them. He wouldn't be working at Duke's residence and would be on a leash at all times, but it was still a good idea to find out how on point Jedi stayed with other strangers around to distract him.

While Greg, still fresh from his difficult and very brief flight, didn't relish the idea of being a stand-in for a veteran needing a service dog, he very much understood the logic behind the choice. This was something that had to be done, and he most certainly wasn't going to let down Jedi, Wendy or Duke because of his own private little drama.

Wendy put on Jedi's service vest before they'd

even exited Greg's SUV at the park she'd chosen for their first public appearance. She handed Greg the dog's leash.

Jedi had been trained to serve the person holding his tether, and this was their first chance to see how he did.

Jedi did so well that they upped his game for Saturday. At Greg's suggestion, they took him to Seaforth Beach, on Jordan Lake, one of his oft-chosen places to get out and relax. But he saw his mistake in suggesting the idea as soon as Wendy came out of her house in some mesh-shirt thing covering her deep maroon bikini top. He hoped to God she wasn't planning to take off the bold yellow gym shorts she had on to reveal the bottom of that swimsuit.

They were going to the beach to walk a dog for business purposes, not so they'd have a chance to go swimming. Or spend a day lounging on the sand.

As evidenced by his own lightweight beige shorts, white short-sleeved shirt and flip-flops. No swim attire for him whatsoever.

And how in the hell was a guy supposed to wipe his mind of the sight of the curves of her breasts, nearly exposed by a tank top as she lay tangled in rustled bedcovers, if their owner kept drawing his attention to them?

By keeping his gaze averted, that was how.

It was easier, once they were out of the vehicle and he had Jedi beside him. Knowing that the dog—and whatever future veteran Jedi was going to help—

was counting on him, Greg relaxed into the man he knew himself to be.

He was there to serve.

Even with sun on his skin, the sound of children calling, laughing, screaming some, and with sand in his toes, he experienced it all through the lens of Jedi's reactions, his behavior.

"The water's beautiful today," Wendy said as they walked not far from the water's edge with the dog between them. There was a strange note in her voice, almost of longing. It caught his attention.

"You come here a lot?" he asked. The forty-minute drive from Spring Forest wasn't bad. It was a little farther from his home in Hendrix, but he still made the trip several times a year.

"I haven't been here in years, not since I was little. I'm shocked by how much I remember it. You'd have thought it would have changed a lot in a quarter of a century."

She made herself sound so old, while he couldn't shake an image of her as a little girl, playing on the beach, like some of the children who were playing around them. He'd been to the beach as a kid, too. Might even have been there on the same day as her.

Would have liked to have known her.

"Your family came here?" he asked, just to fill in the mental picture he'd drawn, watching as a couple of kids approached, looking at Jedi. The dog behaved perfectly, keeping his focus forward, his slow pace steady.

"Not my dad. But yeah, Mom would bring us."

Us? He'd been under the impression she was an only child. The reminder that he didn't know her as well as he'd thought he had was jarring, like a slap in the face.

Recognizing the ridiculousness of his reaction, he walked silently, watching the lake lap the shore, while Jedi marched steadily beside him.

A little girl cut them off as she ran from up the beach, crashing into the water so close by that they got splashed, and then squealed when her belly hit the water.

Again, Greg paid attention to Jedi, looking for a reaction. The dog's big brown eyes were focused on him as they stood there. And when Greg started walking, Jedi and Wendy kept pace equally beside him.

He noticed, though, when Wendy glanced back at the little girl. Saw the distant smile that transformed her beautiful face into something almost sad. She caught him looking at her and turned forward. "My brother used to take me out and throw me straight up in the air to see how much of a splash I could make when I came down," she said then, with a lighter tone. "I'd try to stretch myself out as far as I could, slamming my arms down into the water when I hit, ostensibly to get him soaked, but mostly to make him laugh."

It was a sweet story, but...it was another mention of a sibling. Another reminder that, even though he'd known her for years, he was just now hearing about a sibling.

And he'd just mentioned that he had sisters, what, a few days before? The thought brought him back to reality.

Still, he couldn't not ask... "Your brother?"

"Yeah."

"Older or younger?" He wondered if he was being nosy—but then, she'd asked him the question about his sisters. Surely that meant he could reciprocate.

"Older," she said, with emphasis. "Ten years older."

"It was just the two of you?"

"Yep."

His mental portrait of her grew. A little girl with a big brother, taking her out to the lake to play. It was a nice image.

"I idolized him when we were growing up," she said then. And there Greg was, still wanting to listen. Still interested. "He left for the Marines when I was eight, and I thought I'd die of the loss."

The melodrama in her tone made him smile. And...her brother was military?

"Is he still in the service?" he had to ask.

"No, he left after six years. Joined my dad in his real-estate business. Dad wanted to open a brokerage in South Carolina and have Michael run it."

Jedi continued to walk with them, head high, facing forward, as though proud to be there. Seemingly unaware of the odd course Greg's thoughts had taken.

"You ever throw your sisters in the water?" Wendy turned, threw a grin in his direction, and he thought how beautiful she looked in sunglasses. Hoped that his own tinted lenses kept his expression as placid-looking as it should be.

"Nope," he answered. "I was too busy swimming, trying to see how far out I could go and beat my last time, to pay much attention to my sisters. Besides, they were busy with what I considered to be girly things…"

"Girly things?"

"Making castles in the sand. Sitting in the shallow water digging for treasure…" Maybe if he'd thrown the girls in the lake a few times, they wouldn't think he was such a weakling who needed to be coddled like an invalid…

"I made sandcastles." Wendy's tone was playfully defensive.

"Why do I think they were planned and executed to specification and far enough from the water not to get flooded midbuild?"

A grin and a playful punch to his shoulder were her only responses.

They left him wanting more than just the touch of her fist against his shirt. More of the grin. More often. More of the way his breath caught when he looked at her. More of way his body lit up at even the slightest contact with hers.

Left him wanting more of other things he couldn't

have. Like a future with Wendy always by his side. During good times and bad.

On Sunday Wendy took Jedi downtown for a stop at her office and then a walk on her own. She'd noticed Greg favoring his left leg by the time they'd come up off the beach the day before, noticed how almost dismissive his quick *See ya later* had been when he'd dropped her and Jedi off at home, and figured they both needed a day off from the partner training she'd initiated.

She'd talked to him about Michael. Just the good stuff, but still...

She never, ever mentioned her brother to anyone in the new life she'd built for herself. But there she was, having him in her home, telling him about Michael—she'd even told him her mother had died when she was sixteen.

What was she doing? Really?

On Monday, afraid of how much she was changing, Wendy almost texted Greg to tell him that he needn't show up for his Jedi time. She could reschedule some appointments and be able to get home for training sessions.

Almost texted him.

She didn't text him.

Instead, she managed to calm her fear of letting him get too close by focusing outside of herself. Instead of thinking about her own reaction to Greg, she pushed that aside and thought about the two male figures who were suddenly taking up such huge blocks of her life. Greg's time with Jedi wasn't just for the dog. It was for him, too, and, as of yet, she'd seen no sign that the man had, in any way, formed any kind of ownership bond with the dog.

Greg was doing exactly as he'd said he'd do. Helping her ready Jedi for service to a veteran who needed him.

Greg wasn't a needy veteran. Or if he was, he didn't seem to be willing to admit it. Perhaps she'd been overreacting, thinking that she had to get him and Jedi together.

Perhaps Greg helping Jedi was good for the dog as they'd planned. And nothing more. Where the handsome pilot was concerned, she couldn't be sure anymore.

He hadn't mentioned flying at all that weekend. And she hadn't asked. She'd had no valid reason to do so. Had no dogs that needed flights up north.

In her office Monday afternoon, thinking about Greg when she should have been number-crunching, the ringing of her cell phone brought her abruptly back to the tasks at hand…until she noticed Greg's number on her screen.

"Hello?" Had something happened with Jedi? The dog had shown signs of a weakened immune system due to malnutrition when he'd been rescued and brought to Furever Paws.

"I think something's wrong with Jedi."

Wendy was already on her feet, shutting off lights, reaching for her satchel, as she said, "I'm on my way."

During the drive home, she'd call the veterinarian who'd been watching over Jedi most recently, since Doc J. had relocated to Florida.

And she'd need symptoms to relay.

"What's he doing?"

"Whining."

"Is he lying down?"

"Not really. Right now he's half standing, half lying on me. His legs are on the floor, but the upper half of his body is in my lap."

Deep pressure therapy.

Deep pressure therapy?

Was Jedi trying to offer comfort to himself? Giving himself the therapy he knew to give others when they were stressed?

Or was he…

Had he noticed…

Was Greg struggling?

But the whining…

"What was he doing before the whining started?"

"Sitting here."

"Where is *here*?"

"We're sitting outside… I pulled a lawn chair over under the tree in your backyard. Figured it would be good for him to have some outdoor time."

The backyard, even with city wildlife, could be rampant with bacteria that could harm a dog with fragile health.

"Was he running? Did he get stung?"

"No, he was just sitting beside me, and next thing I know, he's whining. And then climbing up in my lap."

By this point, she was already halfway home. She figured, since Jedi was well enough to stand and offer trained deep pressure therapy, that she had time to assess the situation more thoroughly before calling the vet. She still had no idea what to tell him.

Maybe the dog *had* been stung. His immune deficiency hadn't included allergies that she knew of.

"Is he showing any signs of anaphylactic shock?"

"Not at all."

"You know what they are?"

"Yes. I'm CPR-certified."

Of course he was. And at the moment, that was great news. But it still didn't tell them what had caused Jedi to have this reaction.

Maybe Greg had been distracted and hadn't seen what happened. She'd have to phrase the question carefully. She didn't want to sound like she was accusing him of negligence. "What were you doing right before he started whining?"

"Reading."

"On your phone?"

"Yes."

"Like, a book?"

"I was reading about nightmares as a result of trauma, if you must know..." His truculent tone might have amused her if she hadn't been suffused with chills—and a sense that her plan could actually be working. It was sounding more and more like Jedi's behavior wasn't a sign of something wrong with the dog, but the dog sensing that something was wrong with the human, just as they'd been training him to do.

If she was right, then Jedi might really be able to help Greg. And by proxy, *she* could help this man who'd been a godsend to her and her veterans for so many years.

She was home, already parked, and on her way out to the backyard as she said, "As you were reading, were you feeling some of the feelings you felt the other night, when you had that nightmare after the rough landing in the storm?"

She had to work to keep excitement out of her voice.

"Maybe. I don't know."

At her back door, she saw the two of them, man and dog, sitting, as he'd said, under the lone tree in the yard. Greg's hand moved along Jedi's back, calmly, from neck to hip, long slow strokes, over and over.

"I'm here," she told him, hanging up just before heading over to join them.

Blinked back tears. Of no known source.

And went out to greet the men in her life.

Chapter Ten

Yeah, she had his attention. There was no denying that Greg's mood lightened at the sight of the long-legged, curvy woman with her bangs and braid walking across the grass toward him.

Jedi looked, too. Wagged his tail. But didn't climb his front half down from Greg's lap. Greg continued to pet the boy as Wendy approached—wanting Jedi to know that he was enough. That while he was in training to be a working dog, he didn't have to earn affection.

"He seems fine," she said, her gaze assessing their charge.

"He does now," he agreed. "I'd apologize for calling, but you said to report any behavior that was out of the ordinary. Whining was on the list…"

And he was a man who followed orders—most particularly his own.

"I'm glad you called," she told him, taking a seat in the grass next to the dog, legs together, knees up to her chest. She didn't touch Jedi, though. "There are tones to the whining…one signifies pain, and we listened for that a lot when he first arrived at the animal rescue in such terrible shape. He can't tell us what hurts, when it hurts, how badly it hurts… he can only whine when it gets bad, and hope that we humans can figure it out. There've been no reported accounts of him whining in pain, by any of those of us who've been around him, for six to eight weeks now…"

Greg just nodded to show he was following. She'd already filled him in on some of that during his training session. She seemed to be leading up to something. He waited.

"The other whine is one you and I haven't gone over yet, as it wasn't pertinent to your work with him." Odd how she was looking at the dog, not at him. Not at all.

"I'm thinking that Jedi is even more ready to go to work than we knew," she said, watching the dog. Watching his hand on the dog? He continued to lightly rub Jedi's back as her gaze followed the movement.

"The last couple of weeks before he came here, his trainer had been working with him to recognize signs of distress…specifically to get him ready to be of service to a veteran with PTSD, as a lot of veterans suffer from the stress element as well as other issues..."

His hand stilled. For a second there he felt violated. As though someone had intruded on his right to privacy. His life, his struggles, were his own. He kept them that way. Kept everyone safe from them, too.

He was responsible. To himself. To others.

No one knew...

His promise to himself. No one would ever know. Or need to know. He had everything handled. But now, there was Jedi, unknowingly broadcasting that Greg was in distress.

As anger shot up, Jedi climbed down from his lap. And in the next second, when the untoward emotion had dimmed, as it always did in him, he missed the dog's close presence.

"This could be a breakthrough in his training, Greg!" Wendy said. "We're assessing his ability to recognize and then follow through with trained behaviors, and he might have just shown us that he's got it!"

Her excitement startled him. He'd been thinking about how it affected him, to have his mood and his feelings so obvious to anyone, even a dog—but Wendy's words gave him a new perspective. Was it embarrassing for someone to pick up on his negative mood? Definitely yes. But this appeared to be an important milestone for the dog. It meant the training was working. The mission's success mattered more than his potential discomfort.

"It might be coincidental, but I don't think it's a mistake that you were reading about trauma-induced nightmares—something you've recently experienced firsthand, probably triggering a physical response within you—and Jedi gives the trained behavior to the signals you were giving off. He's supposed to whine, to wake up his owner if they're in the throes of a nightmare or a flashback. For some things, like an impending migraine, he's trained to nudge his owner's hand, to alert him or her to take a pill before the headache has a chance to escalate to full-blown, excruciating pain."

Greg nodded along, only half listening. He could understand the logic behind all of this, see how that kind of training in a service animal could be useful—to others.

"Have you had any other nightmares since that initial one here the night of the storm?"

That last part of what she'd said grabbed his attention because of one word. *Initial.*

She thought the emergency-landing-based nightmare had been a first for him. And why wouldn't she? He was just a wealthy guy who liked to fly so much he volunteered his time with a Pilots for Paws program.

She didn't know what he'd been through. His years of fighting the insidious beast, the secret battle he waged at home alone… All of that was still safe. Still hidden. Just as he wanted it to be.

"One or two," he allowed. No harm in admitting that. He could have crashed and died. It would have been strange if he *hadn't* had a few nightmares afterward.

"So the sensations you felt from those nightmares, they'd be close enough to the surface that reading about them could trigger a likeness."

Yeah. Probably. She seemed so excited about the idea…the most excited he'd ever seen her. "Maybe," he said, wanting to keep her happy.

"And Jedi whined!" She didn't suddenly hug the dog. She didn't want to interfere with his training.

But her smile…the tone of her voice as she said, "Good boy" sure felt like a hug to Greg, and the words weren't even directed at him.

He hadn't been having a nightmare, of course. Hadn't been experiencing any of the violent, fight-back energy he generally woke himself up with after a bad one. But, while reading, he could have been feeling some of the insidious fear that built up to the attack instinct…

And Wendy actually thought Jedi had sensed that in him? That the dog had been responding that way—climbing on his lap, whining at him—as a way of trying to stop the sensations from escalating?

If that was right, if Jedi really had those capabilities, the dog's talents were being wasted hanging out with Greg.

But that was fine, since Jedi was never meant to be his dog. He just had to get Jedi through the training, and then the animal could go to someone who really needed the help. Who wanted and deserved that help in acknowledgment of all they'd suffered as a result of their service. Jedi, in particular, could be a great match for a soldier who came home suffering from PTSD.

That wasn't him. He didn't have the migraines. Or the mood swings.

He'd just been born with the curse of an overly active nighttime imagination that blew his current and past daytime activities out of proportion sometimes.

As dreams, and their shadow side, were wont to do.

Wendy didn't sleep well Tuesday night. Jedi, stretched out on top of the covers next to her, didn't seem to mind her tossing and turning. The dog snored right through a lot of it. He wasn't taught to care about such things.

For his sake, she was glad.

For her own…she just couldn't seem to settle. Not when she couldn't stop thinking about Wednesday's visit between Jedi and Duke. Would it be a step forward in making Greg a believer?

Or was the obstinate man going to deny his own needs for the rest of his life? If that's what he was doing. Could be she was too biased, her own form of post-traumatic stress. Seeing likenesses to Michael because of the nightmare Greg had had in her home that first night. Not because the likenesses were really there.

But he was still having nightmares.

And he hadn't mentioned the plane in days.

She knew better than many how much flying meant to Greg Martin.

If Greg had been up in the sky, enjoying his first love, he'd have said something about it. The guy was always going on about the special freedom being in the sky gave him.

A number of times he'd been after Wendy to go up with him. Even tried to use her service animals to get her to agree, once or twice, when a dog he was transporting was skittish about getting in the plane. He'd suggested that the dog would be more comfortable if Wendy was there. Had even said he had a safety belt in the back if she wanted to sit in the cargo area with the dog.

She'd demurred, of course. Her schedule was busy. She'd known the dogs would be fine in the safe confines of their kennels.

The real reason, which she'd been loath to confess to a man as strong and sure as Greg Martin, was that she was afraid of heights.

Always had been.

Michael had teased her about it, working under the theory that doing so would ease her tension. It was why he'd thrown her high in the air and let her drop into the water, making up the splashing game.

He'd never thrown her high enough to scare her, but he'd nudged her boundaries, trying to help her to push past them.

Later, he'd understood suffering from irrational fear. But by then, he'd been unable to help himself, let alone anyone else. And he hadn't been willing to accept her help. Greg seemed equally resistant to accepting any help. She could only hope that taking Jedi to meet Greg's friend on Wednesday—the dog's first, albeit unofficial, meet with a veteran in need—would show Greg how much he could potentially benefit from Jedi's help himself, in the interim.

If he didn't figure that out soon, it might be too late. After the whining episode on Monday, Jedi would be ready to move on sooner rather than later. Who knew when there would be another dog with training who needed to be fostered? If Greg really needed help to get over the near crash?

And once Jedi was gone, and they no longer had the excuse of training him, would she and Greg go back to only seeing each other when she had a dog that needed a flight?

Or worse, if he wasn't flying, would they never see each other at all?

These were the thoughts that kept her restless all night, right up until the sun started rising and she decided that there was no point in staying in bed. It was a quiet and subdued Wendy who was waiting when Greg came in his SUV to pick them up. They'd arranged to see Duke early, before his prelunch therapy session, and she'd dressed in navy business pants and a cream-colored loose-fitting top for the business meeting she had with a new client afterward.

Greg, who'd be spending part of the afternoon at her house with Jedi, looked much more in place in the vehicle, with the dog, in his tan shorts and short-sleeved pumpkin-hued shirt.

And yet, something about him seemed slightly off. Her mind was fuzzy from lack of sleep, and it took her a minute to figure out what it was.

It was his stance. He was favoring his left leg as he'd led Jedi out to his vehicle. Favoring it *again*, because she'd noticed that that leg always seemed to be the one that gave him trouble.

If she'd been thinking clearly, she probably would have left it alone, but she was too tired for her brain-to-mouth filter to be working. "What's with your leg?" she blurted out about five silent miles down the highway.

"It's stiff."

"Why?"

"I pushed it too hard at the gym last night."

"It's always your left leg," she pointed out, trying to make sense of the puzzle. "You got something against it? Don't push them equally?"

"It's an old injury," he told her. "Tore my quadriceps tendon. Surgery only helped so much…"

Tendons weren't like ligaments. They didn't regenerate. Another Michael lesson. Tendon damage was the reason her brother had lost most of the use of his right shoulder.

She wanted to know how he'd torn it. How old he'd been. If he'd been playing football, and if so, in high school or just a start-up game among friends. But even as tired as she was, she couldn't miss the grimace on his face, signaling his discomfort with the personal conversation. As usual.

"I'm sorry," she said softly. "About your tendon, and for being rude. I didn't sleep all that well last night."

He glanced at her then. "Did Jedi help?"

Odd question. But then she remembered their conversation about nightmares under her tree.

"I wasn't having nightmares. I just couldn't get to sleep. And no, he didn't help. He slept through it all." Or most of it.

"Anything in particular keeping you up?"

She thought about dodging the question. Or making something up. But her thoughts were running slow and sluggish, and when she opened her mouth, there was nothing there to come out except the truth.

"I was worried about you, actually," she admitted.

He stiffened noticeably at that. "What about me?"

"Your flying. I didn't want to pry, but you haven't mentioned going up since the lightning strike, and—"

"I've been up twice."

Well. There you go, then.

She'd been so certain he'd have told her.

Swallowing back hurt, she said, "Oh, well, good!

Great!" she said, starting to feel better as his words sank in. Greg was flying.

She'd been overreacting about his anxiety.

He didn't need Jedi and life was on track.

"Why didn't you tell me?" she blurted, then flushed. What right did she have to ask that question, as though she was entitled to be privy to his inner thoughts?

"Because the flights weren't great." His tone of voice—so raw, so unlike him—had her turning, openmouthed, to look at him.

After a few long seconds he said, "I take off, I land. Not much in between. Not yet. I'll let you know when I'm ready to fly for you again."

She hadn't even been thinking about him flying for her...except that if he didn't, she wouldn't have any reason to see him again once Jedi had been placed.

"You're fighting panic?" She inched the question out slowly, quietly, as though its impact would be less that way.

No such luck. She saw him scowl, and he still avoided even glancing over at her as he said, "And I'm winning."

She hoped so. She really hoped so.

But if he had to struggle so hard every time he went up, at what point did he decide flying wasn't fun anymore? At what point did he just give up? Not just on flying but on everything? On life?

Telling herself that Greg wasn't a quitter, that he

was the last person who would ever give up on anything, helped, but only for a moment.

She'd thought the same thing of Michael. Had been certain of it.

But her brother had lost what he'd loved most. His independence. His ability to control his mind. His career. The things he'd had left—including her—hadn't been enough.

Chapter Eleven

Walking into Duke's room with Wendy could have felt awkward, but it didn't. It felt as though she'd already been there. As if she fit.

"Hey, bro, I brought Wendy with me today," he said and promptly grew uncomfortable, as the familiarity with which he said her name made it sound as though he'd brought her up to Duke before.

When in fact, Greg had been preoccupied with Jedi, who, vested and on his leash, was standing beside him at attention.

"Hey, Duke." Without missing a beat, Wendy walked up to the chair in which the unresponsive man sat, touched his hand for a second, as though in lieu of a handshake, and then stepped back.

Wendy's seeming ease, the naturalness with which she handled Duke's condition, hit him, hard. She'd handled it perfectly. Almost too perfectly. It was as if she'd been there before.

It was possible that it was just from her experience volunteering with Pets for Vets, but for the first time, he wondered what had gotten her involved in the organization. Was there a veteran in her own life who had struggled in the aftermath of a tour overseas? The facets of the woman, things he should have known, could have surmised, just kept presenting themselves to him. Like someone slowly regaining consciousness after a long sleep, he couldn't seem to see clearly enough.

Jedi nudged his hand. Reminding Greg that he had a specific purpose that morning. Yanking himself immediately to his goal, he walked the dog up to Duke's chair and told him to sit.

And then, keeping the end of Jedi's leash in hand, he moved over to the seat he generally occupied, while Wendy sat in an armchair over in a corner by Duke's bed.

"I generally update him on sports scores, the news, that kind of thing," he said then, struggling to find his footing in the strangeness.

"This is your visit, Greg, your call," Wendy said. "I'm just here to observe Jedi's behavior."

And so he sat back, pulled up the week's baseball stats on his phone, starting with the Red Sox, and gave his buddy the rundown—with commentary. Jedi sat, back straight, right where Greg had left him, watching Greg.

How did you get a trained dog to give service to a new person instead of the one who'd trained him? That was a question he was going to be asking the second they got out of there.

He wanted to believe that that was the issue—that Jedi was only responding to him. But he feared that the issue went deeper. Maybe Jedi wasn't responding to Duke…because Duke just wasn't emitting anything for the dog to pick up on.

No emotional shifts.

No changes in equilibrium. So with nothing to respond to, the dog was waiting. He'd sit until Greg gave another command.

Reminding himself that one of the goals of the morning's activity was Jedi's training and experience, he left the young dog on command as he scrolled through some current affairs and read them aloud to Duke.

He was a quarter of the way through a piece about a self-propelled car when he caught a movement from Jedi out of the corner of his eye. A relaxation of his stance. Breaking eye contact on Greg. Maybe he was tired? That would be only natural. The pup had made it nearly half an hour at attention. Proud of him, Greg glanced at Wendy, expecting her to look pleased, as well.

Instead, expression serious, intently focused, she was watching Jedi.

Looking back, Greg froze, not even breathing as he watched the dog nudge Duke's hand. And then push his head up underneath the limp palm.

He could hardly believe it. Couldn't explain it. Had some physiological movement or response inside Duke triggered Jedi's action?

Could that really be possible?

Yeah, his friend breathed and sometimes swallowed liquids and soft foods. He blinked and slept and processed waste. But Jedi wasn't trained to react to any of those automatic actions that everyone did.

More likely, the dog had just gotten bored, was looking for attention.

Because he was still in training. Not ready to go into service yet.

Still, Greg watched it play out, as silent as Wendy now, waiting to see what happened. He didn't speak, didn't want his voice to distract Jedi. The dog was still sitting, so technically, still on command.

It was like Greg's own life was in the mix as he watched, rooting for a dog. Rooting for his friend, despite the odds against him.

Duke's finger moved.

Wait a minute. Greg stared, unblinking.

Had he just seen that?

The slight lift had been almost imperceptible. He wondered if Wendy had noticed it. Didn't want to look away even to get a measure of her response.

There. It happened again. Two fingers this time. Very clearly moving on the dog's head, while Jedi sat, completely still, with his head where he'd shoved it under Duke's hand.

Heart pounding, Greg couldn't tear his gaze away. Was loath to speak, to break the spell, to interrupt whatever was going on between dog and injured soldier.

And so he sat, moisture filling his eyes, and watched a miracle happen.

They weren't even out of the facility before Greg was on the phone with someone named Julie.

Julie?

Holding Jedi's leash as they headed toward the front door, she told herself that she had no business being hurt—or even surprised—that Greg had a woman he'd call to share the incredible breakthrough they'd just witnessed.

The man was inarguably gorgeous. He was also intelligent, compelling, kind, rich… Of course he had women. She used to tease him about it all the time, and he'd never once denied it.

Just because he'd never mentioned this Julie or having a special woman in his life…

But why would he feel the need to mention any of that to her? The most she'd ever gotten him to admit was that he wasn't interested in settling down, but it had been quite a while ago that he'd said that. Maybe this Julie had changed his mind.

Either way, it was none of her business. He was helping her train a dog for service. Just like he helped her out by delivering dogs up north. She was the one who was making more of things than were there.

And whether he shared the miracle they'd shared with her first, or someone else, it was the miracle that mattered.

He'd hung up by the time they were strapped in to his SUV and on the road. They kept talking about what Duke's response to Jedi could mean as they sped down the highway toward home.

Her and Jedi's home.

"The doctor said not to get your hopes up," she reminded him, even as she tried to rein in her own hopes.

What they'd seen—a catatonic man trying to pet a dog—was unlike anything she'd ever witnessed before.

And she would never, ever forget it, either.

"I know. But I know it's more than that. All these years, and no other voluntary movements…and you could tell Dr. Robbins was eager to get in there."

Greg had called the doctor minutes after Duke's hand had moved on the dog. Tests were going to be run and compared to others of Duke's brain-wave results. They'd examine technical things. Scientific things.

But science couldn't explain a dog's ability to sense things.

Or a man's need to bond with animals…

"Julie's on her way there now." Greg's words cut her thoughts off midstream. For a moment, she was filled with confusion. Why would Greg's woman friend—

"She sits by Duke's side every single night, for at least an hour. For years, she's been sitting there, certain that her brother was still in there..."

Her brother.

Emotion flared in Wendy, through her, heart constricted with sadness, and hope bringing happy tears to her eyes.

Julie was Duke's sister. Not Greg's girlfriend.

He hadn't said so. But she knew.

And it didn't even matter as her entire being was usurped by a whole flood of emotions from an entirely different source—a sister with an injured veteran brother who was still alive...

On one hand, she felt a pang, wishing she could be that sister, but she pushed quickly past that and reached for the joy that lay behind it—a joy far more personal than what she'd been feeling since seeing Duke's fingers move on Jedi's head.

Duke was a veteran.

And a brother.

She helped veterans by providing service dogs to them. She didn't think about their families.

But this one had a sister.

And they'd just given her hope.

As emotion overwhelmed her, she turned. "You did good work today, Jedi," she said, hiding herself behind praise for the dog and petting him, because sometimes even the handler needed a bit of service.

* * *

Jedi had sensed something, some emotional change, stress maybe, in Duke. He'd distracted Duke by connecting with him physically. And Duke had responded.

Greg wasn't one for drama. He relied on facts.

But he just knew.

His friend wasn't completely lost to them. He wasn't going to kid himself that he'd have Duke back as he'd once been, but a new future had just opened up for his fallen brother.

Thoughts flew all during the drive home, interspersed with the memory of Jedi pushing his head under Duke's hand. Of Duke's fingers moving. Seconds was all it had taken.

And he kept seeing those seconds, over and over.

Kept hearing Julie's voice as he'd told her. The break. The thanks she could barely utter through her tears.

The hope.

The relief.

He took it all on, soaked it in, was brimming with it as he followed Wendy into her house, Jedi, off his leash, bounding in ahead of him.

She had her meeting.

The responsibility for Jedi's afternoon training session was on Greg, but it was hard to concentrate on the tasks that had to be done.

As pumped up as he currently felt, he needed a long run through the forest on his property. Or, more realistic with his leg, a couple of hours on the machines in his home gym. He needed...

Walking in Wendy's front door, with the sun shining in through the sliding glass door leading to the backyard, he didn't see that she'd stopped midstride, turning toward him, and he nearly barreled into her. He didn't, of course.

He was a man in control, not a bull.

But he didn't immediately back up, either.

He heard part of his name on her lips, but when her gaze met his, so close, she fell silent, mouth open, words there, but not given utterance.

The connection between them seemed almost to vibrate with intensity. They'd witnessed an incredible thing that morning. Just them. No one else had seen...

Some probably wouldn't believe.

But they knew.

"Thank you," he said, his throat tight with emotion again.

"I didn't do anything." She kept studying him, as he did her. Searching each other? But for what?

"You introduced me to Jedi. Saw value in taking him to see Duke..."

"I've never seen anything like what happened this morning." Her words sounded like a confession. As though, until that day, even she hadn't known what the dogs they'd been working with could do.

"I still can't believe it," he told her, and then,

thinking of the moment again, the movement of Duke's fingers, he grabbed her up, hugged her tight.

The immense wave of emotion cascading through him had to go somewhere, and there it went from his arms to her body, in a maelstrom of relief. Of gratitude. Of awe.

Of…something more.

Her body against his, her breasts pressing on his chest…desire flared, hot and blinding. Meaning to pull back, he moved only far enough to meet her gaze. To see the fire burning in those expressive green eyes as he bent his head.

Needing. And seeking.

Her mouth. Her lips, parted. The softness of her tongue. He got lost, taking it all, giving as much back, hungry.

So hungry.

And excited.

He kissed her softly at first, and then with more urgency, the newness of her taste igniting him further.

She gave back as fully, pressing into him, her hands on his back pulling him into her, moaning and moving on him, her breath coming in gasps between their lips.

Until they both just…stopped.

If one or the other of them gave any indication of a slowdown, Greg wasn't aware of it. He was kissing her one minute, just living it, and then he'd stepped back.

And so had she.

"Oh, God," he said, running a hand through the strands of his hair. Smoothing his beard. "I'm sorry, Wendy. So sorry."

He should go.

But he couldn't go. She had a meeting. Needed someone to tend to Jedi.

"What are you apologizing for?" Her breath was still a little uneven, but her tone was not. "Last I looked, there are two of us standing here."

Right, but he'd started it. "I swear, it won't happen again."

Nodding, she straightened her shirt, before meeting his gaze again. Head-on. "I'm not worried about it, Greg," she told him. "Whether it happens again or not…" She gave a shrug. "Neither one of us is looking for anything serious, we both know that, so it's really okay."

Was she really saying it was okay if it happened again?

If he'd made things awkward between them…

"Seriously, Martin," she said, grabbing up her satchel and keys. "No harm done. It was an emotional morning. We're human…"

Her gaze seemed to plead with him not to make too much of it. He couldn't tell if her words were sincere or a cover for troubled feelings.

But because he wanted things back to normal between them, he smiled, told her to have a good meeting, and let the relief flow.

Chapter Twelve

Meeting done earlier than she'd expected, Wendy gathered up her things and was getting ready to turn out the office lights on her way out, when there was a knock on her door.

People in Spring Forest knew that she was always available. It was her unspoken promise to them— one of the conscious choices she'd made when she'd designed her new life, when she'd decided who she wanted to be. These people were her priority, and she would be there for them.

So while she'd been filled with nervous energy to get home to Greg—she went back and forth on whether or not it was to release him from duty and get him out of her space for a bit or to maybe look into the possibility of trying on another kiss to see what happened—she ended up leaving the lights on and answering the door.

Elise Mackenzie, the petite twenty-five-year-old woman who worked at Barkyard Boarding—an overnight and day-care facility for pets—stood there, smiling somewhat shyly. Wendy knew who Elise was, of course, but mostly because of her aunt, Regina Mackenzie, Spring Forest's wealthy self-proclaimed do-gooder, with whom Elise lived. Regina was into everything. Elise, not so much. Wendy had only gotten to know the younger woman since Elise had started volunteering at Furever Paws after the shelter had drawn attention by hosting a puppy and kitten shower earlier that year. But what she knew, she really liked.

In some ways, she and Elise had a lot in common. They kept to themselves when it came to one-on-one personal relationships. And both had lost their mothers before they were eighteen—Elise's mother having passed away when she was just ten years old.

That marked a girl, somehow.

"I was wondering if I could speak to you for a moment," Elise asked.

Before Wendy could pull her door open farther or even give life to the smile starting to form on her lips, Regina Mackenzie came into view behind Elise. Stepping in front of the younger woman, she slipped past Wendy right into the office, leaving Elise to smile apologetically before following her aunt inside.

"Hi, Wendy," Regina said breezily. "I told Elise that we needed to include you on our list of visits today. You'll want to get in at the very beginning on this one so you can get the most bang for your advertising buck."

Her advertising bucks were very few. There didn't seem to be any need to waste money on ads when she had more clients than she could handle sometimes as it was. Whatever these women were selling, she wasn't at all sure she was interested in buying—but courtesy dictated that she show them to a seat on the couch in the small sitting area in her office and offer coffee from the one-cup automatic brew machine on a cart along the wall.

And felt bad when she was glad that they both declined. Normally she welcomed times just like these, where she sat with her friends and visited.

Normally she didn't have a man in her home who'd just kissed the socks off her.

"Bethany told me that you're aware of the ballooning medical and food bills at Furever Paws, especially since the influx of animals from the backyard breeder," Regina started right in, sitting there regally in her summer dress.

"I am." Wendy nodded. "Which is part of the reason I've taken Jedi. As his foster, I'm footing any further medical bills plus the cost of his feeding and have taken over his training, too."

"Yeah, that was so sweet," Elise said and smiled. "But they're talking about maybe having to separate

Salty and Pepper since no one's come forward who is willing to take both of them."

Salty and Pepper were, respectively, a cat and dog duo who were believed to have been the personal pets of the now-jailed backyard breeder. The two were inseparable. And while Pepper was sweet-natured, Salty lived up to his name and didn't seem to like anyone, creating another obstacle to getting him adopted.

"I sure hope not," Wendy dropped to her chair, a wrench in her gut. "They're family. They need to stick together. They clearly love each other, but more than that, they look to each other for security and—" She stopped, realizing that her own emotional past was rising too close to the surface.

"I agree completely, which is why the animal rescue needs a fundraiser," Elise said, coming alive as she sat forward, her long brown hair curling around her shoulders giving her a softness that Wendy had never had. "I think we should—"

"I want to run a dog fashion show as a part of this year's Spring Forest fall festival," Regina butted in, her louder voice overpowering her niece's. "Each dog will have a sponsor from a local business, and all money will go directly to Furever Paws."

Wendy wasn't a fashion-show type of girl, but she could see many of the town's residents getting into the spirit of the thing. "It's a great idea."

"You're a business owner," Regina pointed out as she handed Wendy a piece of paper. "I figured you would want to sponsor a dog, so here are the details, with a sponsorship form at the bottom."

Wendy glanced at the price. "Of course, fine," she said. "But, just so you know, I'm not going to sign up as an accounting business. I'll do it in the name of Pets for Vets."

Looking satisfied that she'd gotten what she'd come for, Regina rose to her feet, Elise jumping up right after her.

"We've got a lot more people to see before offices close for the day," the older woman stated as she opened the outer door of Wendy's office and then turned. "And if you know of anyone else who you'd think would like to sponsor a dog, let me know, and I'll add the name to my list."

Immediately, Wendy thought of Greg.

But then, she was thinking of him pretty much all the time, so no surprise there.

"I'll give it some thought." Meeting Elise's gaze on the way out, she gave the quiet woman a smile and made a mental note to reach out to her more when she saw her at the shelter.

Elise seemed lonely…and Wendy didn't ever let loneliness thrive in Spring Forest if she could help it.

Maybe that was why she'd had Greg on the mind so much. The man was always alone, and Wendy's mission in life was to leave no person behind.

She wanted to believe that was all it was—that that was the reason she couldn't seem to stop thinking about him.

But she knew that wasn't it.

Not really. Problem was, she had no idea what to do with that.

Greg had been thinking all afternoon about the sexiest kiss he'd ever had. Nothing had ever felt as right as Wendy in his arms, matching him touch for touch, kiss for kiss. It had been better than anything ever uttered in a locker room, that was for sure.

And it had been a terrible idea. He couldn't go that route of trying for a relationship—not with Wendy, not with anyone. He couldn't even handle having a pet in his life. He'd never forgive himself if he injured anyone, lashing out during one of his nightmares. The possibility was all too real and all too frightening.

Yeah, Jedi had nudged Greg's hand when he'd been reading about nightmares. Yeah, it was possible he'd been experiencing some of the physiological symptoms of the fear and fight induced from them and that Jedi had picked up on that.

But a dog who could sense nightmares couldn't actually cure the man who experienced them. What if Jedi got too close? What if he got hurt?

No. Hearing Wendy's garage door go up and her car pulling in, he shook his head. It didn't matter how hot that kiss had been or how badly he wanted to repeat it. Dating a woman seriously was out of the question for him.

He couldn't take the chance that he'd get weak,

want to spend the night in her arms and wake up to find himself hurting her.

It happened. He knew of a guy who'd been with him in Afghanistan who'd broken his wife's nose.

The oh-so-hot woman he'd kissed came in through the garage door...stopped midstride when she saw him there and met his gaze.

And he knew she'd been thinking about him some, too.

That she hadn't yet forgotten the kiss. The kiss he'd just decided couldn't be repeated. Not without it leading to something more that would only put her at risk.

All he wanted was to be good to her and for her— to make a positive difference in her life. He couldn't do that romantically, but was there something else he could offer?

And suddenly he knew how he could make her happy. Not by kissing her again. Or trying to start something he knew he couldn't finish.

But by being the man he'd been in her life for the past several years.

Her friend. Her pilot.

Maybe minus the flirting...

"What do you think about Jedi going up with me?" he blurted the question before he could think it to death and change his mind.

Before he could scare himself out of facing a bit of his own truth—and maybe sharing a small piece of it with someone else.

Duke had made an incredible stride that morning, beyond what anyone had expected from him after all this time. If he could do that, then Greg, with all of his capabilities, felt doubly challenged to be his best, as well.

Which meant finding what it took to do the most difficult things.

As caught up as he was with his own internal battle—having just pretty much admitted, out loud, in company, that maybe he needed some help—it took him a second to see that Wendy, mouth open, was staring at him.

"If I've just overstepped, I apologize," he told her quickly, half thinking maybe there was still time to backtrack…to take back any little bit of vulnerability he might have shown her, while also remembering that she'd been the one to suggest that a dog might help him.

A dog.

Not the incredible Jedi.

"Stop with the apologies already, Martin," she said. "I'm just…temporarily speechless. Enjoy the moment."

Cocking his head, he met her gaze.

"I think it's a great idea," she said then, busying herself with rinsing the cup she'd brought in with her and putting it in the dishwasher.

Giving him privacy for his second or two of hot flash followed by cold chills. For the…relief that suddenly made him feel different. A small bit lighter.

"You know, with chances being that a vet suffering from PTSD could also then suffer from a fear of flying," he blew out quickly, trying to cover up any deeper reason she might have gleaned from his request. "The more experiences Jedi has, the more ready he'll be to face whatever he'll be exposed to when he goes to work…"

The way she was looking at him, expression easy, but eyes narrowed, made him tense.

"I just have one request…"

Bracing himself to hear her ask for more than he could give, he was surprised when she said, "I'd like to go up with you. As his handler. He's not fully trained yet—he hasn't been cleared for service. If he gets it wrong…"

Greg would be fine. Jedi would be, too. He knew he could fly safely and professionally. The idea was to do it without fear, without the battle that had taken all joy out of the activity to the point of him wondering if he was ready to be done with his time in the sky.

Wendy was waiting for an answer.

"I'm fine with that."

Standing there, looking at him, her eyes glowing with a satisfaction that went beyond any physical pleasure, she said, "Good. When?"

In a while.

A time in the future.

Greg thought of a song his mom used to listen to. Something about tomorrow never coming. But then he recognized the weakness in his thinking and was ashamed for even having the thoughts.

After taking a deep breath, he ran a mental play of her schedule. And his own. Narrowed down the first time they'd both be free. "Saturday morning?"

Her grin set him on fire again, tempting him to leave pain and fear behind for a few hours of ecstasy. Of hiding.

Making his arms antsy to reach for her.

He reached for his keys instead, wished her a good-night and ran for his life.

To safeguard hers.

Chapter Thirteen

What in the hell had she done, offering to go up with Greg? The reasoning had been completely valid in that Greg seemed to be suffering from a form of PTSD that caused him to feel anxious about flying. Jedi should be able to help him divert panic-related symptoms before they overwhelmed him, but Jedi hadn't finished training yet, was not cleared to work.

Not to mention, Jedi still had his own medical complications. Every test showed improvement, and he was definitely getting closer to full, robust health. But it was still possible that he could come down with a sudden fever while they were in the air.

All true. All good reason to not let Greg and Jedi go up without her. Not that she could fly, but she could take care of Jedi while Greg brought them down.

She could find another, fully trained, service dog to borrow for the morning. One that wouldn't need another human being in the plane. Except that Greg wasn't fully accepting that he needed one. He was bonding with Jedi. He cared about the dog, and there was a foundation of trust. She knew that was a lot of the reason he'd suggested taking the dog up. If he'd been consciously seeking what he needed for himself, it had only been as a peripheral, as in, maybe Jedi could help make the flight more pleasant for him, but he didn't need the dog to complete the flight.

As such, he would certainly reject a fully trained dog there just for his benefit. The only way he'd accept comfort and help from a service dog on his plane would be if that dog was Jedi. And if Jedi was going, she needed to be there in order to supervise.

Yep, all valid reasoning to join Greg and Jedi on their flight.

Only one small problem.

Her damned fear of heights. The curse had even been there when she was a child living with her perfect family, before everything had gone wrong. And while she'd tried to rid herself of the phobia—had even done an online session with a therapist—there was just some baggage that had refused to vacate her premises.

Her dad knew. No one in her current life did.

And she'd be damned if anyone was going to find out.

Which meant, as she sat at work on Friday—a part of her all too aware that Greg was going to be at her house shortly to take Jedi out for a walk around the local park—the rest of her was silently panicking over the idea that she had less than twenty-four hours to mentally prepare herself to be able to actually get on a plane. A small one. With a pilot who might or might not be overly tense and have to give every ounce of attention to getting them up and down safely.

And for her to do so without freaking out.

Yeah. Like she could do that.

Except, how could she not? How could she expect Greg to do something she wasn't doing herself? She, of all people, knew that facing and conquering fear was essential so that it didn't rob you of your best life.

Problem was, she'd already tried. Many times.

How in the hell was she going to climb up into that plane and not let it show?

The outer door of her office suite opened, saving her from the mental back-and-forth that had been plaguing her since the evening before.

And when she saw Elise Mackenzie there—alone, for once—all thoughts of her small irritating situation took a step back.

"I got your message. Aunt Regina is on a call, so I came to collect the money and form for the sponsorship," the young woman said. She seemed different somehow, more relaxed, exuding more confidence, without her aunt barreling in front of her.

Did it mean something that Elise had come by

herself and hadn't just waited for her aunt to finish her call?

"Have you got a minute? In addition to sponsoring a dog, I'd like to be involved in the show if I could," Wendy said, heading toward her seating area, offering coffee, which, this time, Elise accepted.

Waiting for the first cup to brew, she stood at the cart and continued. "I was thinking it would be great to use Jedi. He's still with us, a walking example of the great things going on at Furever Paws, and... I'm fostering him until he's ready to go into service. I thought maybe I'd wear khaki colored pants and a green T-shirt and he could have a fatigue cap and maybe an in-service vest." The coffee was done. She started her own cup and went to deliver Elise's without missing a beat. "I could decorate the vest, you know, with studs or some fancy something, and decorate his leash, too...make it fun and bold and... something colorful, so those watching get the same feeling you get when you watch a parade."

"I love it." Elise's smile filled her face, coming across as thoroughly genuine. And kind.

"We could have donation buckets going around for those watching. That way, the fundraiser would pull in money on the sponsorships and from the viewers." Elise stopped talking to sip as Wendy joined her on the couch.

Fifteen minutes flew by as they discussed various aspects of the doggy fashion show, and then Elise's happy, excited expression faded.

"We'll have to run all of this by Aunt Regina, of course," she stipulated. "The fundraiser is her baby."

"Why are you letting her do that? It was your idea, wasn't it?"

Elise looked surprised. "You...you could tell?"

"Yeah, it was obvious," Wendy replied. "When she talked about it, all she had were generalities. You had the specifics. It was clear you'd given it a lot of thought already. So why let her hog the credit?"

Shrugging, Elise seemed to size Wendy up, as though she wanted to share something but then just shook her head and eventually offered, "With all of her contacts in town, she'll be able to collect double or triple the money I could, and that's what matters most here. Money for the rescues. Security for the shelter."

Wendy nodded. She got it. Agreed even.

Still... "Your aunt does a lot for this town, and I know she means well, but...sometimes I find her a bit...pushy." Maybe she was crossing a line by sharing her opinion so frankly, but she had the feeling that Elise would welcome an ally. Maybe even a friend?

"She can be a bit overbearing," Elise said, her tone soft, "but, you're right, she means well..." Elise sipped at her coffee, focusing on the cup in her hands, but didn't seem quite done speaking. There'd been a tone, as though she had more to say, and so Wendy left space for more, sipping from her own cup for a couple of seconds.

"My dad and Regina's husband were brothers. When my dad got sick, he was in a nursing home for the last few years of his life. He had savings, but not enough. Money ran out. I was just a kid...and Regina was kind enough to pay the enormous bills. He was only her brother-in-law. Not even blood family. She didn't have to do that. But she did. I'm forever grateful to her."

Wow. Wendy had had no idea. This insight left her with new respect for the pushy older woman. And for Elise McKenzie, too.

They had something else in common—an understanding that family wasn't necessarily those whose blood you shared. Instead, it was those who were there for you when you needed them.

Those who wanted you there.

Who needed you.

Like Greg needed her and Jedi?

Was she thinking they were connected like family?

Pets for Vets family. Pilots for Paws family.

The thought settled into the void left by the potential problem her overly inquiring mind had coughed up.

And felt right.

She and Greg were connected as family. Had been for years. And that was the reason she'd committed herself to a successful flight for him on Saturday, in spite of her own issue.

Her feelings for him—not to mention her feelings about the *kiss*—were inconsequential next to that.

What the hell? She had to be kidding.

"Did she talk to you about this, Jedi?" Walking around the end of a card table set up in a corner of the spare room, Greg took in the array of studs and jewels and what looked like sewn letter appliqués surrounding the dog's service vest.

"Do you see what she's doing here?" he asked. It was quite a surprise. While he knew Wendy liked bold colors—as evidenced in the throw pillows and wall hangings in her home—she'd always kept that out of her fashion choices. It was kind of nice to see her going for something so visually striking.

But...

She was training Jedi to work for a veteran. He couldn't think of a single one, male or female, who'd choose to be accompanied all the time with the glitz and glamour to the overboard extent she had laid out there.

If she was decorating a Christmas tree...it'd be great.

An injured veteran, one who'd already probably be somewhat self-conscious about needing full-time help, was almost guaranteed to not want to be attached to the visual equivalent of a Christmas tree every time they went out the door.

He sure as hell wouldn't want to be.

Jedi, as intuitive as he was, didn't seem to understand the higher points of fashion. Maybe it had to do with the color blindness of dogs. Or maybe he just hadn't grown up enough to have developed a keen fashion sense. Either way, the dog just stood there, eyes questioning, completely focused on Greg. He didn't even seem to notice the service vest.

Which made Greg quick to change his stance and his tone as he said, "You ready to get to work? Wendy's going to be home soon."

And Greg was hoping to be gone by that time.

He'd see her the next morning. At the hangar. He was taking a breather from her until then.

Or so he'd planned.

A few minutes before she was due to be off work, a full twenty before he expected her home, he was just feeding Jedi his last treat for successfully completing his charge, when he heard the door open from the garage into the kitchen.

Damn.

He needed a break from the sexy accountant slash dog foster mom.

Less than a minute after he'd heard the garage door, there she was, all gorgeous in her beige pants and white sleeveless blouse, with that braid hanging over one shoulder, her fingers working the end of it. As soon as she spotted them, she headed out the screen door to join them on the back porch.

Jedi, who'd been officially dismissed, bounded up in puppy exuberance to greet her. Probably telling her, in his own way, that he'd successfully completed every single one of his tasks and had even gotten to take a walk in the park.

And at Wendy's affirmation that Jedi was a good boy, Greg figured the message had been received. Not a word had been said, but she was giving Jedi his due.

But as she bent down to touch noses with the dog and ran her hands along the sides of his neck, Greg lost his good humor.

Did she have to be pouring affection out so liberally in front of him?

Before his body had a chance to forget the feel of those hands on his own neck?

Was she trying to kill him?

Which reminded him: if she was planning to have Jedi dressed out to work the next morning...

"What's with the jewels and all the other decoration on the service vest?" he shot at her.

Standing, she frowned. "What?" Then, as her brow cleared, she said, "You saw the table in the spare room?"

"Jedi was barking at a guy riding a bike, and I followed him into the room to see what was going on."

She knew the dog went from window to window across the front of the house—traveling between rooms as he did so—whenever he thought a bicycle might be anywhere nearby.

"Yeah, that's for Furever Paws," she said a little absently, paying most of her attention to the dog, her back almost completely to Greg. "With all of the unexpected rescues and subsequent expenses from that backyard breeder, they're really starting to feel the crunch, so they're setting up this doggy fashion show as part of our fall festival to serve as a fundraiser."

A dog fashion show.

The vest was for a show.

The rush of relief felt good. Until it lowered his defenses against her. And left him floundering out there for a moment. "I could help," he announced. Help the shelter. Or even just with Jedi's expenses.

Made sense. He had the money. And thinking about it took his mind off other things.

Like wanting to kiss her again.

"You want to sponsor a dog for the fashion show?"

Uh, no.

"I'm putting up the money on behalf of Pets for Vets," she said. "And showing Jedi."

"I'm not interested in showing a pet in a fashion show, if that's what you're asking." And then, getting some of his sense in order, he said in a calmer tone, "I can pay for a sponsorship, though. On behalf of Pilots for Paws. Anonymously. Or just make a donation to Furever Paws."

He should have thought of making a donation already. He knew Jedi had been in bad shape, knew that his medical expenses had been high. "I owe Jedi big-time." His voice evened out as the idea gained momentum. "After what he did with Duke…"

Wendy turned, her face unsmiling as she studied

him. How could those green eyes express so many thoughts and feelings just by looking at him?

Was he imagining things? Making up the caring he thought he saw there?

"I think a sponsorship in the name of Pilots for Paws would be a great idea," she said, sounding odd, a bit dry-mouthed. "Not only would it help raise money for a very worthy program, but it will generate publicity for the pilot program, too. We could maybe do an article for the local paper about our two programs working together to get service dogs to veterans across the state and beyond."

Yeah. Publicity. A business move.

Her justification tied things up in a neat and clean fashion. Because if they were "working together," as she'd so perfectly put it, how could they be anything more?

They couldn't. And they shouldn't.

And, as he got the hell out of there, he took away a lesson from the exchange.

Probably best to keep things strictly business between him and Wendy.

He'd much rather that than have things get so awkward between them that they'd choose not to see each other anymore.

And he had a pretty strong hunch that if they didn't get things under control, that was just where they were headed.

Chapter Fourteen

Don't look down. Stay outward-focused. Think of Greg and Jedi, not yourself. Pay attention to how they're doing, not on what the plane is doing. Touch Jedi if you start to get scared. Look at him.

If all else fails, think about kissing Greg again.

The strategies ran through Wendy's head as she drove her SUV toward the airstrip where she and Jedi were meeting Greg.

The dog, having no idea what he was in for, sat calmly beside her, watching the world speed by them, seemingly without a care in the world.

He'd started his life neglected and seemed happy just to be cared for. Anything else, he seemed to take in stride. A powerful lesson to her.

"Maybe I should adopt you myself," she told the young dog. When he turned those big brown eyes on her, looking at her as though he could read her thoughts, she nodded. "Yeah, I know. You're made for bigger stuff than hanging out and being my family member," she told him. "You're going to give someone who's been hurt their best life and be their family member."

But she couldn't leave it at that.

"You know I wish it was Greg, don't you? If he needs you like I think he does?"

The dog glanced at her and then immediately back to the front window.

She took that as a *yes*.

For some reason, as she turned on the road Greg had directed her to, she actually felt stronger after that exchange than she had since Thursday night. After making a couple of more turns, she found his hangar along the dozen or so that were spaced out evenly to the left of a single runway.

It helped that they were the only ones out there that early so his SUV couldn't be missed.

She saw the plane, too. Knew it immediately as the one she'd delivered dogs to countless times over the past several years.

And immediately looked away.

She'd never felt frightened or intimidated at the sight of the plane before. But then, she'd never been about to go up in it on any of the previous times they'd had their encounters.

And her little drama wasn't even on the radar that morning, in terms of important events about to happen.

Was Greg ready?

Feeling jittery? Worried?

Had he had a nightmare the night before?

Would he let Jedi help him?

Funny how it didn't occur to her to wonder if *Jedi* was ready. She wasn't at all concerned about his ability to help Greg.

"You're going to learn how to fly today, Jedi!" she told him, her tone upbeat and confident. Exactly what he needed from his handler so that he would go into the event calm and confident himself. The pup fed off her energy, viewing the world in the way she framed it for him. She knew that.

And for that reason, she had to keep her own stress level down to nonexistent.

If she didn't, Jedi could fail his test, fail Greg.

And she wasn't going to let that happen.

Not because of an irrational fear that had no basis in reality.

She had no demons to fight, no traumatic event that had caused reason-based fear.

She wasn't Michael.

Or Greg.

But, oh boy, Greg was Greg, in full flavor, as he smiled at her when she got out of her SUV. In black shorts, a white T-shirt and tennis shoes, with his longish hair windblown and his beard reminding her of how his lips had felt against hers, he was too delicious for words.

She'd probably have dropped right there on the tarmac for him if he'd asked…if she hadn't had Jedi there, of course.

And more important business to tend to.

But the idea was undeniably intriguing…and she toyed with different versions of it while Greg, all business and giving no indication of any nervousness, finished preflight checks, and they gave Jedi time to familiarize himself with the inside of the small plane.

With Greg in his seat, she stood on the step just outside the plane and watched the dog. Jedi explored, exhibiting the curiosity of a kid, and then sat on the floor, just behind and between the two front seats.

"You've got a full back seat there." She said aloud what she'd just noticed. "I thought it was only cargo space."

"Usually it is. The seat is removable."

A back seat.

Or a godsend, depending on how you looked at it. "I'll strap in back here," she said then, climbing in. "I'll be close if he needs me, but out of the way."

Out of both of their ways, she thought as she buckled herself in.

The flight was about Greg and Jedi.

Not about her.

"You strapped in and ready?" Greg turned in his

seat to look at her, sounding confident, and not the least bit nervous.

The headset he wore gave him a commanding look that tweaked at her lower parts, and she let herself go with it. "Yep," she looked him in the eye. Smiled.

When he smiled back, exuding testosterone as his gaze held hers, she was pretty sure he knew where her thoughts had landed.

Greg made it out to the turn that would take him to the runway as he had countless times before. His mind on the flight path, the sun coming up fully in a cerulean background and the woman in his back seat.

He stopped there, waiting for the okay to take off, and, as had happened every time in the past week, his stomach knotted. There was no joy. No anticipation.

His headset crackled, signaling a voice coming on, and as he reached with both hands for the yoke, his right hand jutted upward and missed.

Jedi. Nudging him from behind his arm. As though the boy could read his mind.

As Greg corrected his hand's position after the dog's mishap, he got his permission to take off, turned on the runway and up he went.

Perfectly. As though he'd taken off a hundred times before, he reminded himself with a touch of sarcasm.

Times a few.

The route was short. Out to Jordan Lake, circling around Seaforth Beach and back. Chosen for Wendy's benefit.

As a surprise to her.

He figured if she was giving up the little bit of free time she had to help Jedi complete his training, then he'd give her a little gift as recompense.

An aerial view of a wonderful childhood memory.

As he flew, he pictured her face as he'd seen it on the beach, relaying her memory of her older brother throwing her in the air. And realized that he was smiling.

Doing what he loved and smiling.

Life didn't get any better than that.

Ecstasy and peace, right there together. Once again.

Having Wendy and Jedi along for the ride… They'd done this for him. With him. An odd concept for him, being on the receiving end of the giving. But it felt right.

Less than an hour after he'd secured the plane's door for takeoff, Greg pulled the aircraft back into the hangar, his adrenaline pumping full steam.

Smiling so big it hurt, he turned to check on Jedi, who, other than that first bump, had been quietly absent from the cockpit, and to let Wendy know that he was back in action. Ready to fly for her program.

He'd take the next dog up and all the ones after that.

Bring them on…

The words ready to burst off his lips got lost after

his first glimpse of her. She was smiling at him, but her lips were trembling. As was the hand that held out Jedi's leash to him.

The dog half lay on her lap.

"What's wrong?" he asked, his stomach sinking. Had Jedi been in trouble and he hadn't known? Hadn't noticed? "What happened? Did he get sick?"

The floor, the empty parts of the seat, showed no evidence, but...

"He did great!" she said, the influx of enthusiasm in her tone clearly fake. Forced. She hugged the dog as she set his front paws on the floor, every movement a little off her mark. "Didn't you, boy?"

Greg led the dog up front and then out. And then he waited to help her down.

When her fingers grasped his, tight and trembling, he stared.

"You were scared. You didn't trust me to be able to do it." Had he just sounded hurt?

Did she actually think he'd have gone up, risking her life and Jedi's—and anyone's on the ground who could have been hit by a crash—if he hadn't been sure he could do it? He hadn't gone up the first time, solo, until he'd been sure he was capable of getting the plane back down safely. He'd spent time in the cockpit, on the runway, found his flight sense before he'd gone up. After that, his struggle had been enjoying the experience. Not letting fear stop him from wanting to fly. Surely she'd have known that about him.

Letting go of his hand, she took a couple of steps toward the hangar entry, her back to him, and then turned and said, "On the contrary, Greg. I trusted you so much I went up in spite of my ridiculous fear of heights."

With that, she called Jedi, led him to her SUV, climbed in and, without even a wave, drove away.

He couldn't follow her.

She knew he couldn't follow her since he had to tend to the plane.

Watching her vehicle pull out onto the main road in the distance, he stood there, feeling kind of… insulted.

Not for the reason he'd felt insulted just a minute ago. Despite what he'd thought, it was clear that Wendy truly did trust him as a pilot. There was a kernel of comfort in that. But it was outweighed by the proof that she didn't seem to trust him as a friend.

It was okay for her to insinuate herself into his well-being, to insist that he spend a night on her couch so she'd know he was okay, but she wouldn't let him even see her struggle with a normal, common fear?

What was up with that?

He was affronted. But also wanted to comfort her.

Who better than he to help someone through a little bout of irrational anxiety?

Because he was proof that you could get through it.

Seriously, was he no more to her than another one of her…her…clients?

He pulled himself up short at that. Did he *want* to be more than that? Of course he didn't want to be a project or an object of pity for her, but did he want something else? Something other than what they had been for the past few years? They were work partners.

What more did he want?

Maybe…maybe they could be work partners who helped each other through an occasional moment.

Like the fear of heights trigger she'd suffered that morning.

He could envision it. Liked it.

And thought of the way his body had lit up by a mere playful touch of her hand on his shoulder. And then that kiss…

Not a work moment. In any fashion.

So his plan had flaws.

But he absolutely could not ask her to be a friend and work partner who occasionally had sex with him.

No matter how much interest the idea held for him.

There were some things he could not have. Same for him as everyone else. Just a part of life.

So he thought of what he could have. What he'd just regained. His joy of flying.

He was ready to take the plane up again. A longer flight. Maybe to Charlotte. His parents were arriving that day to visit his sister who'd recently announced she was pregnant with what would be their first grandchild.

And, he was sure, so his mother could make sure he was really okay since he hadn't been talking about the various flights he'd taken recently—normally the only thing he spoke about during their weekly conversations. After thirty-three years with them, he knew how it all went.

Knew, too, that things would go easier on him if he went to them before they took it upon themselves to drive over to him.

And also, maybe he missed them and wanted to see them.

Sunday would be better. Give them a day to recover from the long flight. To get settled in. Catch up with his sisters over coffee. So, with a full day ahead of him to fill, he could head to the ocean, do a flyover, maybe land and get some lunch, be back before dark...

His phone rang.

Wendy. Staring at the name on his screen didn't make it go away. Didn't make her appear, either.

"Yeah?" He had to know that she was okay. She'd been upset when she'd left.

"I suck at other people seeing my weak moments."

Leaning back on his plane, he looked out at the sunlight reflecting off the tarmac. "If this morning was anything to judge by, I'd have to agree with you there."

"You had a great morning!"

"You didn't." Did she understand how much that upset him? He hated the thought that she'd been struggling and he hadn't even noticed. Had she felt like she couldn't reach out to him? That he wouldn't understand? Or worse, had she thought he wouldn't come through for her?

"I didn't want to ruin your high."

"I can feel good about my accomplishment and care that you're struggling at the same time. One isn't exclusive of the other."

"I make pretty decent empanadas."

Greg paused, bewildered and with no idea how to respond to that non sequitur. "Good for you?"

"Okay, Martin, I'm sorry. There. All right?"

"Damn. I thought you were getting ready to offer to make me dinner to celebrate my being back on your pilot roster, and all I get is an apology?" He grinned, a little tense, awaiting her response.

"I can only have you over if you accept my apology. Jedi's rule. Otherwise, he's coming to stay with you." He was pleased to hear a teasing note in her voice. It felt like they were back on solid ground.

"He said that."

"I guess you'll have to come here and ask him for yourself if you don't believe me."

"What time are the empanadas going to be ready?"

"Six."

"Tell Jedi I'll be there. Us guys have to stick together."

Greg hung up on her, that trip to the ocean now not only his own private celebration of enjoying the

sky, but also a way to pass the interminable hours
that lay between him and those empanadas. Between
morning and the evening hour that allowed him back
into Wendy's company. He grinned his way to the
ocean and back, feeling a high he hadn't known in
years, made a perfect landing back home, bedded
and secured his aircraft, and went to give hell to his
business associate.

Because he could.

Because she wanted him there.

Because…in the moment…he wanted to be there.

And because he wanted to tell Jedi what a good
boy he was for taking care of her that morning.

Chapter Fifteen

She should have nixed the wine. Standing in her kitchen, with Greg looking so fine in a lightweight button-down shirt that hung casually over his waistband in a way that seemed designed to draw her eye to his fly, she knew that a glass of wine before dinner hadn't been the best call. The black jeans he had on did nothing to hide his goods, and she couldn't seem to stop herself from looking at them.

And glanced up to see him watching her in turn.

"Malbec," she blurted. "The wine's Malbec."

He might have asked. She couldn't be sure.

He'd said something when she'd handed him the glass.

"Dinner will be ready in a couple of minutes..."

And that's how the next half hour went, too. Her noticing him. And trying to pretend she wasn't.

Jedi sat at the corner of the table, his gaze moving back and forth between them. Greg cut a beef empanada in half, held it out for the dog. "Don't get used to this, but you did good today, Jedi. You deserve a treat."

She looked away. Knew it wasn't good for the dog to have table food but also knew that spoiling him a bit wasn't going to hurt. He was on prescription dog food to build his weight. And Greg was right that he deserved a treat.

Beyond that, had Greg just acknowledged...

"He helped you," she said aloud. The fact was too important to be left unsaid. "You had a moment there before we took off, Jedi nudged you, distracted you, brought you out of it, and you ended up having a great time."

Greg was shaking his head, chewing, but still shaking his head.

"You *did*," she insisted. "I saw it on your face when you turned around."

"I'm not denying that I had a good flight," he said after a quick swallow. Picked up another whole empanada and said, "But that's not the same as saying he *helped* me. He knocked my hand off the yoke, actually, which was the opposite of useful. But he comforted you, and that's what I was rewarding him for."

What? Okay, yeah, the soothing weight of Jedi

on her lap had kept her from a full-out panic attack up there in the sky. That and focusing on Greg's thighs, keeping her gaze firmly planted inside the plane. But…

"He supported you, too, Greg." She couldn't let it go. Couldn't let him continue to think he hadn't benefited from Jedi's assistance.

And if his nightmares were continuing as she feared they were, she couldn't let him lose his chance to be Jedi's owner. Based on what she'd seen with Michael, the nightmares were only a part of what could follow.

Swallowing another bite, following the food with a sip of wine, he said, "I'm not saying he wouldn't have been a help if I'd needed it. I'm saying I didn't need it."

He wasn't exactly her brother. Michael had known he needed support. He just hadn't believed there were any resources to be had for him. Greg refused to accept that he wasn't okay, that he needed a service animal. Which meant he wouldn't agree to adopt Jedi for himself.

And the end result was the same: a man struggling on his own.

"You're going to sit there and tell me—in front of Jedi, who knows—that you weren't feeling any panic at all, no unease, when he nudged your arm?" She leaned forward, put her face close enough to his that he'd have had to sit back to look away from her.

He blinked. Frowned. Shrugged. His fork suspended over his nearly empty plate. "It wasn't panic." The words took a long time coming.

Hearing them was worth the wait.

"Call it whatever you need to call it, Greg. It was starting, just like it has ever since the night of the storm, and Jedi's nudge took you out of it."

"Maybe. But…"

Shaking her head, she held his gaze. "No *but*s. That's Jedi. That's what he does. Just like when you were reading about nightmares. He senses. He *knows*. I can't explain it. But I've seen it in other dogs, not as young as him, but still…"

He had to get it.

She couldn't accept any other option.

She played her trump card. "Just like with Duke." Then, because she knew it would hit its mark, she even admitted, "And with me, this morning. That was why he moved out of the cockpit. He knew you were fine, but that I wasn't."

When Greg took another bite, relief flooded through her. She had him. Taking a sip of wine, she hid her smile.

"Why didn't you tell me you're afraid of heights?"

Wendy choked on the wine.

She'd opened the door. Had admitted that she'd had a problem that morning that Jedi had helped with. He wasn't letting her shut him out.

"Come on, it's only fair to tell me. You're all up

in my stuff," he said, enjoying the best tasting empanadas he'd ever had.

"I'm not up in your stuff."

"Of course you are." He gave her a *whatever* look. Did she really think she was going to waylay him? "You have been since the night of the storm. All over me to let Jedi, or some other dog, help me out. And maybe, just maybe, for a minute there, you were right." He'd give her a carrot. Because he was going to take a bushel of them. "I told you I was still having moments of panic when I tried to fly."

He chose his words carefully. It wasn't easy to say this, even if he was just telling her what she'd already guessed. He definitely wasn't interested in getting into the rest of it. She had no idea that the emergency landing wasn't the beginning of his struggles with panic or with nightmares.

And those weren't fixable. No dog could get in his head and stop the images from coming at him. And no way he'd ever risk hurting someone…

He was getting off track, while she sat there silently, sipping her wine.

"Now in turn, I want to know why, considering the fact that I was about to take you up in a very small plane, you didn't tell me you were afraid of heights."

"Because if I'd told you, then you wouldn't have taken me up."

"You don't know that. It wasn't like your fear was going to hurt anyone but you. You weren't in charge of the plane or of anything other than yourself. If you'd wanted to try to beat your fear by going up, I'd have understood that. Just like you understood my battle with panic these past weeks."

"Okay, no, that's entirely different," she said, her voice gaining strength. She wasn't eating much, though, and the dinner was excellent.

"How is it any different at all?"

"Because your fear was reality-based. You'd been through a traumatic situation. There was reason for you to feel afraid. I don't have that kind of excuse. I've been scared of heights for as long as I can remember—and for no reason at all."

"Fear's fear. It's never reasonable."

Shaking her head, she held his gaze. "But there's nothing that triggered it. You've got trauma because something happened to you. Something that would rattle anybody. My fear…it comes from nothing."

"So, what? That somehow makes it not…what? Not legitimate? Not deserving of understanding?"

He sipped. She sipped. They stared at each other.

"Why do you think you're not worthy of the same help you think I'm worthy of?"

Her mouth opened. Her eyes closed.

He couldn't let it go. Too much wine. Too much… everything where she was concerned. "Wendy."

"No."

"Yes."

"I'm not enough." Her words were stark. As real as it got. But that didn't mean Greg could follow the logic. It sounded nonsensical to him. Not enough? Wendy was more than enough—always.

"What in the hell does that mean?"

Shrugging, she shook her head. "Look at my dad. He goes on a six-month cruise that'll have him gone over the holidays, and he doesn't even tell me he's going until the day before his departure. Even then, he makes no effort to try to see me before he goes. I wouldn't have known if I hadn't called him. I'm not reason enough to hang around." There was no self-pity in her words. They could have been talking about the weather.

Biting back the string of swear words that came to him, Greg took a breath and said, "If you ask me, *he*'s the one who's not enough."

He had his own father issues, having felt as though he'd disappointed the old man when he'd refused to maintain a career in the military, breaking a hundred-year family tradition. Deep down, Greg knew his father would have understood if Greg had opted to change tracks—even if he'd taken a desk job, or opted to work at the academy. But it wouldn't have been enough for *him,* and Greg knew he'd had no choice but to leave.

Yet even as he told Wendy her father wasn't enough, he couldn't say the same about his own. Despite his disappointment, the general had been there for him. Not saying much, but supporting his choices, his efforts, in any way he could.

"Maybe," Wendy said slowly. "It's not just him…

Anyway, you're right. I should have told you that I was afraid of heights before we went up."

"Jedi knew. He helped you, didn't he?"

He grinned at her, and she smiled back. "Yeah, he did."

"So…maybe we could go up again? This time you sit up front with me, and Jedi rides in your lap. I'd like to show you the ocean from above, but low enough that you can see the dolphins swimming."

"Are you asking me on a date, Martin?"

He had to look away. Couldn't look away. "No, because that would ruin things," he said, rawly honest.

"I agree."

"But I have been wondering about the possibility of a physical encounter that was only for the moment…if we're both on that same page?" For all his fighting them, the words just fell out.

Her head tilted, her mouth curving into a sexy smile as a knowing look entered those light green eyes. "I've been on that page since Wednesday…"

"The kiss." He licked his lips, looking at hers.

She licked hers back.

And he was done with empanadas.

For all their heat, he undressed her slowly—as she did him. Her fingers trembled when, standing beside her bed, she unfastened his buttons one at a time, wanting them undone, but not wanting the undoing to be over.

"You have the most beautiful pecs of any man

I've ever seen." She ran her hands over his chest. His shoulders. Smooth skin. Crisp dark hair.

"You've seen a lot of men, I take it?" His tone was teasing. She wasn't sure if he was digging for information or not.

"At the beach, Martin. Swimming pools, going for a jog during the summer..." She licked his nipple. Planted her lips against him. "I've had a few lovers," she admitted. "Few and far between."

Would he find that a turnoff? They were keeping this light. Maybe it would make him uncomfortable to hear that taking a lover was a rare occasion for her and that he was one of very few.

"I'm not into hopping beds, either." They were the sexiest words she'd ever heard. She couldn't look at him, though. Couldn't let the connection become deeper.

"No one current, then." She did want to confirm that one.

"Nope. You?"

"Uh-uh." Her voice slid down his chest to his belly button, traveling over him right along with her lips. And tongue.

He tasted like salt. Smelled of clean, musky man.

And just an inch lower, jutting up in wait...

Delicious shivers passed through her as he reached over her, running his fingers along her back. She felt him reach his destination, the slight pinch on the fabric and her body tingle with wanting as her breasts fell free. He didn't stop there, though. Moving down her back as seductively as he'd crawled up it, he grabbed the bottom edge of her shirt and pulled it over her head.

He lifted her. She stole a glance up at him and saw that he was gazing with adulation at her honey-colored breasts.

That look—like he'd seen a piece of heaven—melted her.

No one had ever looked at her like that.

And that was her last coherent thought before he pulled her down to the bed with him and encased her in a haze of red-hot physical delight.

Lying side by side with Wendy, her leg wrapped over his waist to accommodate their still-joined bodies, Greg wanted to close his eyes and drift with her. Just until his body could recover enough to have a third round.

The condom he was wearing saved him from making the mistake.

He couldn't fall asleep. Most particularly not after his emotions had been in such high gear. Didn't seem to matter if his emotions stemmed from sexual arousal, excitement, joy or horror beyond imagination. Any kind of heightened feeling increased the chance of a nightmare.

And the aftermath of sex—even the most incredible he'd ever had—still brought reality.

Pulling out of her before the condom failed, he

slid away and into the bathroom adjoining her bedroom, as he had already after their first round.

And, as before, she held out her arms to him, inviting him back to bed, when he reentered the room. Standing there naked, gazing at her sleepy, sated expression, he fought the strong temptation to take her up on the offer. "I'm sorry to disappoint, but I can't do a third time," he said, sitting on the side of the bed and reaching for his shirt. "Not without recovery time."

He ached, not from physical exertion, but from the tension that was his constant companion since being medically discharged from the army. From the responsibility that gave him a life sentence of aloneness.

His leg ached a bit, too, but that he could easily ignore.

"You could recover here."

He couldn't turn around. Couldn't look at her. Couldn't afford the temptation.

And yet he knew that he *had* to look at her. She deserved that much.

Standing, shirt hanging open, Greg put one foot and then the other in his pant legs—foregoing the underwear, shoving them in his pants pocket—and faced her. "I can't," he told her as she sat up, propped on pillows, holding the covers to her chest. The position reminded him of the first day he'd let himself into her home and found her in a similar position.

Plus the skimpy tank top. Minus the covers.

"Why not?"

"I can't fall asleep here."

The moonlight didn't provide a lot of illumination, but he met her gaze, telling her with every part of him—his voice, his eyes, his dressed body—that he meant what he said.

There was no other option.

No plan B.

She might be willing to risk getting hurt, but he absolutely could not risk hurting her. He'd been born to serve and protect.

"Why?" The response was too long coming. Husky sounding.

"You know why."

"Actually, I don't. You think if you fall asleep here, what we shared is going to turn into something more than in the moment?"

That, too. Maybe he should go with it. But no, she deserved his honesty.

"The nightmares," he reminded her.

"You're still having them?"

He hadn't in the past few days. But he might that night. Or the next. Or the one after that. The guarantee was that he *would* have them again. Years of history with them had taught him that. And no way was he turning that night into a history lesson.

"Yes," he told her. Keeping it simple.

They were business associates. Having a moment of sex.

Top-of-the-wow-meter sex. But still just sex. Not

a relationship. Not love. Those weren't options for him. Not when there was a risk of her getting hurt by everything he carried with him—everything that roiled within him that he couldn't erase.

Love was no more of an option for him than it was for Duke, locked up in his own mind, yet in an entirely different way from Greg.

Still, the end result was the same. Both of them slept alone.

Greg reached for his shoes.

Chapter Sixteen

She didn't follow him out of her room. Didn't even get out of bed. Not until she'd heard the front door close behind him.

Throwing on a robe, she traipsed to the front of the house, checked that he'd locked the front door behind him. And then, with Jedi at her side, she went straight back to bed.

She didn't cry. Not then. And not the next morning when she woke up to an instant replay in the light of day, either.

If she'd had any kindling of hope that there could be more between them than a purely physical encounter, that she actually wanted more out of her life, he'd just snuffed it out.

But she'd never really believed she could have that anyway. That's why she wasn't crying.

She wasn't even slowing down.

Yeah, she'd wanted him to stay. She'd wanted to cuddle up and fall asleep in her lover's arms. To wake up...not alone.

She'd done that part, at least. Waking up not alone.

She didn't need a permanent man in her life.

What she needed was a permanent dog. A family member who wouldn't leave her until nature separated them. She'd had her life so planned out, had followed the plan, but hadn't known about some of the happiness she'd been denying herself.

Hadn't known how empty her house was until she'd opened it up to Jedi. And to Greg, of course, but she didn't need them both to be permanent fixtures.

One could come and go as life took him. Leaving her world intact.

The dog, though, the idea of having one of her own had taken root. She couldn't get one fast enough.

Maybe one of the newborn pups at Furever Paws?

She tried to keep her mind focused on the idea of puppies, but in spite of herself, her thoughts continued to drift back to Greg as she went about her usual Sunday-morning routine. He needed a dog in his life, too. Specifically, he needed Jedi—she was certain, now that she'd confirmed that the nightmares weren't going away. But she knew she couldn't force him to accept that. She'd put Jedi in his path, and that was all she could do. He had to want to help himself, and it looked like he didn't.

He didn't want a service dog. And he didn't want her. Not for anything more than a dalliance that didn't even last a full night. Fine, then. So be it.

She talked it through with Jedi as she took him for a long walk downtown Sunday after lunch, getting in more public hours for him. The conversation was intermittent, interspersed with various other chats with people they ran into along the way, all who wanted to greet Jedi.

She couldn't let them, of course. He had on his vest and couldn't be petted or coddled while he was working, but he did his job well, sitting at attention, focused on her, as she socialized.

"Anyway, we'll be seeing him tomorrow," she told Jedi as he jumped in the passenger seat of her SUV after clocking ninety minutes of public time. When the dog gave her a soulful glance, which she interpreted as expressing doubt, she quickly reassured him. "Greg's not going to let you down," she told Jedi. And then, as she climbed in on the other side of the car, she added, "He's not going to let me down, either. Not when it comes to service. Greg's all about service."

And she admired that about him so much.

Even more so an hour later, when she got a call that a seeing-eye dog that was to be delivered to a veteran in the Raleigh area had been reassigned to a young woman up north who was just getting out of rehab that afternoon. They needed a pilot as soon as possible.

Luckily, she'd put Greg's number on speed dial when he'd agreed to help her with Jedi.

Even luckier, he picked up before the first full ring even had a chance to sound. "I'm sorry." The unusual greeting stopped her for a second. She sat there in her idling SUV, still parked in front of her office, with Jedi beside her, his nose up to the air-conditioner vent, without a quick comeback.

"I know leaving like that last night was uncool," he continued, "and—"

She cut him off before he could get any further. "Where are you?"

"At the airport."

"Coming or going?"

"Going, why? If you need something, I can re-schedule. What's wrong?"

Damn. She'd been trying to sound as normal as possible, but she must have missed the mark. Maybe that was to be expected when she was struggling to evade mental flashes of his voice in her ear as he'd entered her the night before.

"A twenty-two-year-old veteran who was blinded by an explosive is going home today, and the seeing-eye dog they had set up for her is no longer available. We have one who was headed to a veteran in Raleigh today, but he's insisted that we take her to the other vet instead. He's been blind for twenty years and is fine to wait until we can find another dog for him.

This girl… It's critical to her emotional health that her homecoming be as easy as possible, that she feel as independent as possible…" She was rambling. He wasn't interrupting.

"Like I said, I'm at the airport," he said when she cut herself off. "How long will it take you to get here?"

She glanced at the clock on the dash. Just before one. And there she sat, wasting precious time. Putting the vehicle in gear, she said, "Give me a few to get arrangements finalized, and I'll call you back."

"I'll be here."

It was as simple as that. Because it was work. And they were business associates. She could always count on him to be there for the cause.

She liked knowing that.

And if she would have liked for him to be there for her in other ways…well, she'd get over it. Eventually.

Relieved that Wendy wasn't holding the night before—his walkout—against him, Greg hung up and pulled out the lawn chair he kept at the hangar, taking a seat to wait for her call.

As he sat, he dialed his mother, rescheduling his trip to Charlotte for the following day. He was scheduled to be with Jedi then, but now that they knew the young male could handle flying, the dog could head down with Greg. His mom, when she heard the reason for his delay, was all cheer and happiness with the changed plans.

Greg was pleased with the new arrangement as well, especially when he thought about having Jedi as a firm, inarguable excuse to not be able to extend his stay overnight. There and gone was the best way for him to handle time with his family.

Schedule change handled, Greg...just sat. His mind wandered back to Wendy and his relief that sex hadn't ruined things between them.

That they were still who they'd been, in spite of what they'd done the night before.

But...why wasn't she at least a little bit bothered by how their time had ended?

He sure as hell had been.

All the way home, after he'd worked out for half an hour in his home gym, taken a long, hot shower and gone to bed, he'd still been filled with self-loathing—and regret—for walking out on her.

The look on her face when he'd taken one last glance back as he'd left...it had been more than enough to prove that he'd hurt her.

Not that you'd have known it by the way she'd sounded on the phone that morning.

He'd been trying to figure out how to make it up to her. How to get her to be okay with the little he had to give.

How to help her not take his limitations personally.

And it appeared she wasn't taking them on herself at all. Not trying to help. And not taking offense that he'd left her lying there naked in bed after having sex with her. Denying her request to lie there and hold her afterward.

Was it…was it because she expected to be denied? There was something she'd said earlier…about not being enough. It added up with some other things she'd said to him before, not to mention the way she acted sometimes, as if she was surprised at the idea that someone would pay attention to how she was feeling. It seemed like that fear—no, not a fear, a *conviction* that she wasn't enough—was planted deep inside her.

Had he, by leaving her bed so soon, unwittingly fed her sense of not being enough? Was she so accepting of her own view of herself that she hadn't even blinked when he'd gone home?

He could have it all wrong.

But he didn't think so.

Standing, hands on his hips, he stared out to the runway and the horizon beyond, not liking the view his mind's eye was showing him. A giving, beautiful-inside-and-out woman, holding her arms out, being denied…and not seeming at all surprised.

How could she possibly be okay with that, process that?

By treating him as though nothing hurtful had happened between them?

She should be pissed, demanding more for herself. Telling him off for not at least staying long enough for some cuddles before he had to go. Or demanding that he keep his hands off her in the future. Instead, she had cut him off before he could even finish his apology.

By the time she called to let him know she was on her way to pick up the dog and would have it to him within the hour, he'd reached a point of no return.

The woman had to know that she was worth more than gold. And that she had to start standing up for herself. To fight for herself as hard as she fought for others. Greg was bound and determined to make sure she learned that lesson.

Even if realizing what she deserved meant Greg never got to touch her again.

"You on your way to get the dog now?" Wendy heard a definite edge to Greg's voice on the phone. Was he having second thoughts about going up?

Or second thoughts about working with her?

If she had to, she'd drive all night to get Lady to that young veteran up north, but flying would make everything so much faster and easier...

"I am," she said, shoring her internal resources to handle whatever was coming.

"And you can talk?"

"Yes."

"Good. I'd like to know why you think you aren't good enough."

What in the hell? Talk about coming out of left field! Still, she could tell from his tone that he wasn't going to back down. There was no point in trying to redirect the conversation.

"I told you, my dad…" She couldn't finish the sentence. No way was she some kind of victim who sat around feeling unworthy because her father was a bit self-centered and had never been all that much of a family guy.

He'd adored her mother.

And he'd tried, with her and her brother. Had been a pretty decent dad when times were good, when their family was easy. It was when things had gotten harder that he'd started to truly pull back.

"Your dad, what? What did he do to you?" He sounded as though if he found out, he'd go hunt the man down and make him pay for it.

Her senses on full alert, she frowned. "Not really driving-in-the-car conversation, Martin."

Not casual-friend conversation, either. Or even friends-with-benefits.

And yet, there they were, having it.

"You'd rather sit down together face-to-face and have it?"

A big *Hell no.*

She swallowed. And almost smiled. He knew her pretty well.

Tough conversation definitely needed a step-back approach. A little distance between her and the person she was talking to made it easier to open up. And maybe, in light of the fact that they'd had sex—no, not that—but in light of the fact that she'd been all up in his business with the anxiety and nightmares resulting from his emergency landing…

"My father didn't do anything to me," she told him. Which was kind of the point. "After my mother died...he basically just vanished. He paid the bills. Made sure I had what I needed physically." But pretty much left her to raise herself during the last three years of high school.

And so what? She'd been fed. Warm. Secure. Provided for. She'd had a car. Nice clothes. Lived in a good neighborhood. He'd been sober—which was more than her mother had been those last years after Michael.

And he'd made it home more nights than not.

"And from that, you gather you aren't enough?"

"This really isn't in-the-moment conversation," she said then, turning into the empty parking lot where she was due to meet the trainer to take custody of Lady. He didn't know she'd just parked.

"What aren't you telling me?"

"Um, I'm thirty-three years old. There's a lot of things I've lived through. Most of which you don't know."

"Why do you think you aren't enough?"

Damn, the man was tenacious.

She knew that, of course. He'd been persevering when he'd risked his life to deliver a dog with a storm coming on. And pretty determined to get back up in the air again when his life's passion was threatened. She just hadn't expected him to aim that doggedness at her.

"I'm at the meet point," she said then, wanting

him to think she had to go. That the other Pets for Vets volunteer was there waiting for her. But wait— then he'd be expecting her sooner… "Theresa isn't here yet."

"Why do you think you aren't enough?"

Tempted to hang up on him, she held the phone silently to her ear instead. Swallowed hard for a second time.

And said, "Because I wasn't enough to live for."

"You're talking about your mother?"

Only in part, but okay. "Yeah."

"I assumed she died of cancer, or something else terminal. You were so young…"

"She drank herself to death." Literally. And that last day, she'd managed to consume three full fifths of one-hundred proof whiskey.

"That couldn't have been your fault."

"I didn't say it was. What I said was that I wasn't enough reason for her to live."

His silence after that revelation was a little unnerving.

"Sorry that you asked, now?" She posed the question laconically. Giving him a chance to shrug off his mistake and change the subject.

"No, I'm sorry that you find her substance abuse in any way indicative of her love for you."

He wasn't letting it go. Just couldn't let it go…

This man was so gorgeous. And giving. And generally amazing. But also incredibly infuriating. Why couldn't he just let it go?

Why had she let him into her home? Into her bed? What was it about him?

"You still there?" He sounded concerned.

He'd know she hadn't hung up. His phone would show that they were still connected.

"It was my brother, okay?" she blurted, tears stinging her eyes as she opened them toward the sun shining down. So she could be forced to close them.

Oh, God. Why did life have to hurt so badly?

"Michael? What did he do to you?" That tone was back—if she didn't explain right away, he'd be out for blood.

Didn't know that he needn't bother. Michael had already been hurt in the worst way possible—and he'd done it to himself.

"He killed himself, Greg. He was hurt in combat. Came home a completely different man than the Michael I knew. And then he killed himself. Knowing I would be the one who found him. Now, can we drop this, please? Theresa is pulling in."

Because that was how life worked, most of the time. If you got to the end of your tether, someone came out of somewhere and gave you a string to hang on to until you could get ahold of yourself. There'd been so many strings held out for Michael, but he'd refused to take them. Wendy had made the opposite choice.

People her parents had known, teachers, friends' parents, a counselor or two…they'd all been strings for her once upon a time.

And they were all the reason she tried to spend every waking moment of her life being that for others.

The rest—the getting to the end of her tether part—that was why she couldn't risk her heart another time. She wasn't ever going to let herself get to the point where something mattered so much that losing it made her not want to live.

She should be thanking Greg, really.

He'd just reminded her of everything she'd almost forgotten while within his arms.

She wouldn't forget again.

Chapter Seventeen

The flight would have been a complete joy, if not for the heavy heart he took up with him. And brought home with him, too.

Wendy hadn't even gotten out of the SUV when she'd done her drop-off. She'd driven up to the hangar, he'd walked out to meet her, she'd rolled down her window, given him the folder of papers, told him the dog's name was Lady and thanked him profusely for helping on such late notice.

Throughout all of that, she didn't look him in the eye.

Anyone watching would never have believed him if he'd said he'd had sex with the woman the night before. Twice.

He wanted to be affronted, insulted…something other than heartbroken for her.

But the truth was, he understood completely.

Wendy's brother had killed himself. And she'd found him. Then she'd lost her mother to alcohol and her father to his need to escape grief by hanging out with other people. Of course she wasn't going to yell at him for leaving her. It was what she expected. And the next part of the dance was for her to move on, as she'd always had to before.

He couldn't even fathom.

He texted Wendy, as she'd requested, when he got home late that afternoon. Heard back from her immediately, with a thumbs-up and smiley face. Akin to responses he'd received from her in the past.

He needed to call. To drive into Spring Forest and see her.

But that was what *he* needed. *She* needed him to leave her alone. He got that.

At least she had Jedi there with her. Greg had never been so thankful for a dog in his life.

And before bed, he looked up Marine First Lieutenant Michael Steven Alvarez. Found an obituary, first for a Michael Alvarez, in Raleigh, at about the right age and time of death. From there he found that the man was survived by a sister named Wendy, that he'd been a lieutenant in the marines and that his middle name was Steven. From there he found a very old social media post, too, back from the days of one basic service for such things and read about how a fourteen-year-old relative had come home from school and found him dead from a self-inflicted gunshot wound. Apparently the relative had been keeping him company every afternoon since his medical discharge months before.

She'd only been fourteen years old...

Her mother—she'd told him that she'd been sixteen when her mother died.

And a picture started to form.

Based on the look on her face that day at the beach, the tone of her voice as she'd talked about her brother throwing her up in the air to land in the water and splash him, she'd been the baby in a seemingly solid family. And then at fourteen, she had lost any sense of innocence she'd ever had.

Followed by the slow, tragic loss of her mother.

And her father, Steve Alvarez...he'd lost enough to make any man lose his mind. But he'd had a young daughter left at home.

One who'd needed him so desperately...

Greg got it all loud and clear. Whether or not Wendy would ever be able to open her heart up fully to anyone again still remained to be seen.

But opening it to Greg? An injured vet who still suffered from violent nightmares?

It wasn't going to happen.

But more than ever, he knew that he had to be her friend. To be one person in her life who was always there when she called. Even if the calls were just to fly dogs up north.

Pets for Vets. Her dedication to the organization all made sense now.

And he knew he was going to have to tell her the truth about himself. To tell her the real reason he hadn't dared stay in her home the previous night.

To let her know that it wasn't because she wasn't enough.

But because she was.

He couldn't tell her, though, until he'd done all he could do to make his own life right. He couldn't go to her as another broken man with hidden issues but, rather, a man who was doing all he could do, who would *always* do all he could do, to accept who he was and make the most of the life he had.

That thought firmly in mind, he loaded Jedi in the plane with him on Monday—he'd let Wendy know by text that he was taking the German shepherd up while she was at work—to have the requisite lunch with his family, take a better look at the actual sonogram his sister had texted him an image of and, then, to have a talk he should have had years before.

Monday morning, Wendy was finishing up the second-quarter books for a chain of secondhand clothing stores when she got a call from the one paid employee with Pets for Vets, Victoria. Hired by the volunteer board, Victoria's official position was executive director of the nonprofit, but she served the organization in every capacity from receptionist to supply manager.

One of their veterans had passed away over the weekend, leaving the dog they'd placed with him, a nine-year-old golden Lab—aptly named Goldie— without a home.

Goldie's age made her more difficult to place as her future years of service were limited. The owner's family had talked of sending her to a shelter, but if they did so, then, again due to her age, her chances of adoption would be limited.

"I said I'd take her while everything is sorted out," Victoria relayed from her car phone. "I'm on my way to Winston-Salem to get her now," the director continued. "But with Jasmine, I'm not sure I'll be able to keep her for more than a day or two."

Jasmine was a rescue who'd been too skittish for service. Unfortunately, she was also unable to get along with other dogs as she'd been trained nearly from birth in illegal dogfighting.

"I'll take Goldie." The words were out of Wendy's mouth before she considered any part of their consequence. She'd find a place for her—definitely not in a shelter. Goldie deserved better. "Do you need me to come get her? I have an appointment at four, but I can drive out after that."

She listened as Victoria, who was relieved to avoid any possible run-in with Jasmine, told her she'd bring the older dog to Spring Forest. After they hung up, Wendy wondered what in the hell she was doing. She couldn't take the dog to Furever Paws. Not with all of the puppies and the dwindling funds.

But she was already responsible for a dog. Thankfully, Goldie got along well with other dogs—as did Jedi. But her house…

Seriously, what was wrong with her all of a sudden? Opening her home, her life up first to Jedi, then Greg, and now Goldie, as if letting others in was what she did.

While Wendy's thoughts were rambling toward Panic Road, Victoria confirmed that she'd be at Wendy's office no later than three and rang off.

And just like that, Wendy had a dog that wasn't on loan.

Lunch at his older sister's house had been…the usual. Loud. His sisters and mother all vying to control the conversation, finishing sentences for each other, cutting each other off. Him nodding or shrugging while he filled his stomach with culinary delights. And his father, also eating heartily, smiling in between bites.

"Bunny and Birdie told me they thought you were favoring your leg a little bit when they saw you," his mom said just as he'd filled his plate with a second helping of…everything. "I was worried the crash had caused more damage, but you seem to be walking normally. Is the leg giving you any—"

"Mom!" His youngest sister cut in. "It's not as if he'd tell you if it was. He always says he's fine so let him eat…"

"We need to ask," older sister piped in. The birth

order mattered, he'd determined, on how much weight the others gave each other's comments. "If we don't ask, it'll seem like we don't know, or notice, or care..."

Greg, with an eighth of his plate already re-emptied, glanced at his dad, who was sitting back, coffee cup in hand, smiling as he glanced from one speaker to the other.

And so it went.

Jedi was introduced as what he was, a service dog in training that Greg was helping with as part of his Pilots for Paws program. The pup ate up all of the attention given to him, wanting to be in the middle of everything, greedily snatching up every piece of table food offered to him, and sitting quietly anytime anyone wanted to pet him. He ran in the yard and then came over to be a part of things when Greg's sister showed everyone the sonogram. It was too early to determine the sex, but everyone was happy to toast to the future of the firstborn Martin grandchild.

By the time Greg left his sisters and mother, Dianne, in the kitchen baking chocolate chip cookies for him to take back with him, he heard them both talking about getting dogs.

He'd told his father he'd like a word. The old man was waiting in the den.

Greg left him waiting there while he went out to the rental his mom and dad had driven out to the airstrip to pick them up. He'd left Jedi's service vest—his cue that he was working—in the bag on the back seat.

And he wanted a moment to look at his phone without an audience. If Wendy had texted…

She had not.

A couple of minutes later, when he entered the den in his sister's home, he walked in with Jedi, vested and on his leash.

"Time for his training session?" the elder Martin asked, looking at Greg over a pair of readers as he set aside the book he'd been reading.

"Well…yeah, actually, it's training time," he said. He'd already told his father, in a phone call, about the training schedule. And the older man had just given him a last-minute out.

A reason to be walking in with a working dog.

It was an out he wouldn't be taking.

"But that's not why I wanted to talk to you—with Jedi." He sat down on the end of the couch closest to his father's chair.

His father's steady gaze didn't waver. It never did. The old man just looked at you, and you knew you had to be perfect or you'd disappoint him. And good luck trying to sneak anything past him, because he never missed a thing. Not one iota of a thing.

Which was why Greg had never spent a night in the man's vicinity in the years since his discharge.

"It's been suggested to me that I could use a service dog," he said. "I've slowly begun to suspect that I was offered this chance to work with Jedi as a not-so-subtle way to get me to see how he can help me. And I further suspect that if I want him, he will be with me permanently." He was going on pure conjecture there, but he hoped to God he was right on that last part.

If not Jedi, another dog. But Jedi...

No, if he was actually going to consider having a dog, he really wanted Jedi. The abused animal trusted him. Was secure with him. Did his best work when Greg was around—and Greg trusted him, in turn. Trusted his instincts and his dedication. Jedi was committed to service, just like Greg. They understood each other.

Randolph Wesley Martin showed zero reaction. None. Zip.

How did a guy live up to expectations that couldn't be met?

"I'm pretty sure I have PTSD, Dad."

Horror filled him as he heard what he'd said. There was a part of him that felt like he had to get out of there. To get up in his plane and fly away. But before that feeling could take over, Jedi's nose filled his palm. Just a slight movement. Someone who didn't get it wouldn't even have noticed.

Another small nudge from Jedi, and he found his air. And with it, he found the strength to keep talking.

"Ever since I got home, I have moments... Well, they aren't a big deal, the moments, because I can control them. If I distract myself, they disappear."

Just like the fear. The confidence that filled him as he spoke the truth dispelled some of the otherworldly darkness that had descended seconds before.

"But the nightmares…" He shook his head. "I can't control them."

"Are they still as bad, son?"

What? Openmouthed, he stared at his father. He'd just made two very huge announcements, and his father could have been reading his book for all the change in his demeanor.

"On and off." A somewhat irritated shrug accompanied his answer. "Worse since…the incident a couple of weeks ago. I got caught in a storm, had to make an emergency landing…"

No telling if his father had actually heard the details, even if his mother had shared them.

Randolph nodded, chin jutting. "I'd imagine that's the kind of incident that would bring them on."

Shaking his head now, Greg stared at his father. "I don't get it."

"Get what?"

"I've just bared my soul to you, told you this monumental thing, and you just sit there…"

"If I coddled you, would it make you feel better?"

"Hell no!"

"Exactly."

Oh.

"And while this conversation has been a long time coming, the information isn't a surprise."

"You knew?"

"You don't get to be a general in the army without recognizing signs, or without acquiring acquaintances and friends who talk to you."

Of course not.

"Why didn't you say anything?" He had to ask the question, but he knew why. The same reason Greg hadn't brought it up before now. His inability to handle the stress of disappointing his father had frozen the words in his throat. He'd believed—and maybe his father had believed, as well—that if they didn't talk about it, they could pretend there wasn't this rift between them.

"It had to come from you, son."

"You didn't say anything because then we'd have to deal with the fact that I'm your biggest disappointment," he said. "A hundred years of Martin lifetime service ended with me."

Randolph's eyes sharpened, almost into slits with pinpoints, and they were trained like a perfect shot on Greg. "Don't you ever, ever, put words like that into my mouth." The older man's tone was succinct, biting, sharp, without his raising his voice at all.

It was a tone Greg had never heard before. And for a second there, he pitied any man under Randolph's command who'd ever had it directed at him.

He stood up to it, though. He was going to be the best he could be—even if it was so much less than he should be, less than he and his father had once thought he'd be.

"I can't keep hiding from the truth, Dad. I'm sorry if it upsets you, but…"

The look in his father's eyes softened noticeably. As did the tightness around his lips. Randolph was shaking his head even while Greg spoke. The older man leaned forward, bringing his face just inches from Greg's as he looked him in the eye.

"Listen to me, Gregory. I have never, ever been disappointed in you. Not ever. And most definitely not since you've returned from Afghanistan. I thank God every single day for the man you were, the man who helped pull his friend out of ashes, who risked his life to give his brother a chance to live. And I thank him for the man you've become."

Stunned, Greg just sat there. Completely lost. After a full minute, he admitted, "I don't get it. I'm nothing I was meant to be. I'm not serving and protecting my country. I'm not fighting those who are threats to our nation. I'm not giving my life for my country. I manage money. And get lost in the clouds…" He stopped. Then continued. "And I didn't do such a hot job of saving my friend's life, either. It should be me in that facility, not him…"

Randolph didn't move, pat Greg's knee or take his hand, but the look in his eye, his closeness, felt like a touch. "It wasn't your life, son," his father said as quietly as ever. "I couldn't be prouder of how you served in the army, but it wasn't where you belonged. Not your calling. Everyone has their own purpose. I like to believe you're living yours."

"But…" He couldn't fathom his father's words. Couldn't accept them. Couldn't let himself stray from what he had always accepted as the truth of what he was. And what he wasn't.

Sitting back, his father watched him, with no undue emotion. Just watched.

As he always had.

After a long moment, while Jedi sat unmoving beside Greg, Randolph just started to talk. Calmly. Evenly. "They say that oftentimes an accusation aimed at someone else covers the fact that the accuser is actually guilty of the deed himself." The words sat there. Niggling. Not getting in. "Did you ever consider, Greg, that maybe you're the one who's disappointed in you?"

Hell yes, he was disappointed in himself. He was disappointed that he'd failed his father. And probably his grandfather in his grave. Who wouldn't be? He'd let down the Martin family name…

And…there.

Truth landed.

Feeling lost, like he didn't know himself, Greg wasn't sure what to do next. So he sat. Quietly. And his father sat with him.

After a lot of minutes passed, Greg started to pet Jedi. And another while later, looked at his father. "You've known all along."

One nod was what he got in response.

"And you've been keeping an eye out, waiting…"

"Hoping."

"Because you knew I had to get here before I could be helped."

"Maybe."

He sat silently for more long minutes. Not ready to move.

"In full disclosure," his father finally confessed, "I will admit that some of your mother's nagging was a result of my suggesting that we needed to know what you were up to now and then…"

The chuckle that came up out of Greg didn't hold much humor, but there was some. And for the moment, it was enough.

Eventually he stood, feeling like a different man. He was not healed, but maybe he was finally heading to a better life. At the very least, a better understanding of himself. "I have to get back," he said, wrapping Jedi's leash around his hand as the young dog stood at attention beside him. Ready to learn from him. To…serve him?

Reaching out his free hand to his father, he held on to the tight clasp, realizing where the real wealth in his life lay. "I'll see you tomorrow." He was flying back down to take his father up for an hour—something they'd decided while waiting for his mother and sisters to call them to the table for dinner. Randolph had always wanted to be a pilot, but his army and family responsibilities hadn't given him time.

Greg had become what his father couldn't be. The army, Duke's fate—they weren't his life. Flying and managing nonprofits were.

Randolph picked up the book he'd been reading. "Hooah," his father said to him.

"Hooah," Greg said back, feeling more like the man he'd once thought himself to be—even walking out of there more broken than he'd wanted to believe he was.

Hooah. That stood for loyalty. Always. He'd always had his father's loyalty and always would.

It was time he had his own.

Chapter Eighteen

"I don't know who's going to be at the house when we get there," Wendy said, glancing over at the sixty-pound golden Lab sitting on the seat beside her.

Jedi's seat.

Goldie's seat.

Whoever-needed-it's seat.

"I texted Greg about you, but he hasn't replied, and I don't know if he and Jedi are back in town yet."

The Lab was watching her, her ears twitching. So Wendy kept talking. She wanted the dog to feel comfortable. Secure. Cared about. Losing her owner of many years… Goldie was grieving.

She felt the dog's sadness. Understood it. And wanted to help make it better.

"Jedi's just a pup. Not even a year old yet, but he's smart and loving, and I think you'll like him." She prayed the dogs got along. Until she found them owners, the dogs would have to cohabitate.

Other than handing over the dog stuff, she hadn't spoken to Greg, except by text, since she'd told him about Michael. Was dreading doing so. If he acted like anything had changed, treated her differently...

Who was she kidding? They'd had sex. Things had changed. Truth was, she'd be open to doing it again. But only if they could stay on track as friends only, outside of the occasional night together.

Did she dare hope that telling Greg about her brother had given him deeper understanding as to why friendship was all she ever wanted—with anyone?

Since he was so adamant about living alone himself—to the point of refusing to spend the night after sex—could there be a possibility that they could pull off a long-term friends with benefits thing?

She'd never known anyone personally who'd done so, but she'd seen it on television. Read about it in books...

Turning onto her block, she saw the familiar SUV parked in front of her house. And her mood picked up. She couldn't help it. She was glad he hadn't just dropped Jedi and taken off. Him doing so would have been a sign that things weren't normal between them.

"They're here," she said to the older girl beside her. She pet the dog's head, then with both hands braced behind Goldie's ears, she leaned over and kissed the bridge of the golden Lab's nose. "We'll find someone who needs you, Goldie," she said, pulling back just enough to look the dog in the eyes. "Okay?"

Goldie's tail gave a slow wag, the first that Wendy had seen, and Wendy took it as a sign that everything was going to be all right.

The talk Greg had planned for Monday after work didn't seem appropriate with a new dog in the house. He'd bought steaks for Wendy's grill, had potatoes in the oven, a salad already made, all in the name of honoring a friendship that mattered a whole lot to him. It was all there, the makings of a memorable dinner—minus the wine and candlelight that he'd specifically left off the menu. He'd been planning to surprise her. To be honest with her.

And then in she walked alongside a calm, perfect-specimen golden Labrador with the saddest eyes he'd ever seen.

"She's just lost her owner," Wendy said quietly, as if the dog could understand her words. "Her name's Goldie."

The dog looked at him but didn't venture over to say hello. Or back up when he stepped forward. Running a hand over her head and down her back, Greg said, "Hello, Goldie. You want to meet Jedi? He's eating," Greg explained, looking up at Wendy. Given his health issues, Jedi's eating was priority.

Always. The boy was gaining weight, but they couldn't afford to go backward. Especially if he was going into service.

Goldie didn't seem to mind not being met at the door by a fellow canine. She walked away from Greg's hand on her back, moved slowly around the living room, surveying and smelling, and sauntered into the kitchen.

Smelling his potatoes?

"I...have dinner underway," Greg said. And quickly added, "Not with an eye to anything romantic. Just...I have a proposition—nonpersonal—that I'd like to discuss with you." Whoa. Getting way ahead of himself. The idea was meant to come last, after the rest of what he had to do. It was the glue that would put them back together.

Nodding, Wendy gave him a brief glance but was clearly more interested in the dogs than in any idea he might have brewing. "Good. I'm hungry," she said, almost as an afterthought.

Following her into the kitchen, he saw why she was so distracted.

His potatoes hadn't been what had drawn Goldie's nose. Jedi, in the laundry room off the kitchen, had been the object of her attention.

The boy stood over his almost-empty bowl, head turned to look at Goldie, ears perked up tall, tail still. And Goldie, with her head slightly lowered, seemed to be trying to get a whiff of what was in Jedi's bowl.

Oh, God. Was this a fight ready to happen?

He moved forward with purpose, steadying his pace so as not to escalate what could only be growing tension in the room. He had to get the boy out of there before something awful happened. More likely instigated by the German shepherd whose natural instincts would be to protect his dinner.

Aware of Wendy behind him, noting her silence, he deduced that she was waiting for him to act. He was a protector. One trained to de-escalate tense situations. And if a fight ensued, going into battle was what he did.

Each thought brought him a step slowly closer. He was aiming for Jedi. The dog he knew. The boy who knew him. Who obeyed him.

As Greg drew near, almost close enough to grab for Jedi, Goldie's tail started to wag. Slowly, small back and forth sweeps. And Jedi…finished his dinner.

For whatever reason, the two had decided to tolerate each other. To get along.

Leaving Greg more certain than ever that he had to find a way for him and Wendy to do the same. To be who they were, deal with their complicated feelings for one another in a way that worked for both of them and, above all, continue to get along. The dogs, along with the veterans they helped, needed them to do so.

With Goldie and Jedi lying close but perpendicular to each other on the floor between Wendy and

Greg's chairs at the table, Wendy tried to relax. To let herself enjoy the moment, the company of two smart, nurturing dogs in her home, along with a friend over for dinner.

It was just all so odd, so not her, that she couldn't find a way to just be with it. She kept most of her attention on her plate. The food was good. Impressively great steaks, actually. And yet every bite was a challenge to swallow.

She wanted wine.

Greg had poured ice water with lemon so she didn't feel right helping herself to something else.

"How long are you keeping her?" he asked as he tackled his steak and baked potato with the same gusto he'd given to her empanadas and his chili.

"Just until I can find an owner who needs her," she answered, a little distracted as she grappled with the idea that they were having their third meal together, in her home, in a matter of weeks. Like they were… together or something. Roommates or…dating.

Or friends who were raising and training an abused pup, she amended silently. Then, to that end, she said, "She's teetering on being too old for service but still should have at least five more years in her. For her to live her best life and feel most wanted, she should go to someone who needs a service dog, but who's maybe older, slowing down some, just like she is…"

She didn't know who that would be—no one came

immediately to mind—but she'd put energy into it, sending out feelers, until she found someone.

Before his steak was gone, Greg set down his knife and fork crossways on his plate. He'd barely touched his salad. The actions, strikingly unlike him, made her uneasy. They were doing well. Ignoring the sex and the humongous revelation she'd made and had been regretting every second since. Was he about to break the status quo?

To hell with the water. She got herself a glass of wine. Offered him one.

Only one bottle in the house. Ever. Her rule. She didn't budge on it. And never drank when she was out. Living alone, she knew she would have to drive herself home.

He accepted her offer but didn't sip from the glass she gave him, and her heart sank further.

"I've misled you a bit, Wendy, and I'm deeply sorry for having done so."

Oh, God. He was dumping her. From a relationship they weren't even having. Unless friends with benefits counted? Though, technically, they were friends with benefit. One time. And he was dumping her.

She sipped from her wine, welcoming its calming effect, and set the glass down. Quickly putting her hands in her lap to hide their trembling.

"The night of the storm, the emergency landing— that wasn't my first nightmare."

What? Blinking, she turned toward him, frowning deeply. "I don't follow."

"I've been suffering from violent nightmares for years."

Wow. She hadn't seen that coming. And had no clue why he was suddenly baring himself to her.

Because she'd told him about Michael?

Was this some kind of quid pro quo?

Arms folded, she sat there. She should be saying something. His pause clearly indicated that. But first, she needed him to finish.

"I've never told anyone..."

Still frowning, she sipped her wine again. Quid pro quo, then. Okay, she could see where he was going with it.

"Was there an initial cause?" she managed to ask, getting on board with the program. They were sharing why they were safe with each other, living in the moment only. Why what they had could never be anything more.

"I'm told they call it PTSD." His words were delivered in a deadpan tone. It matched the expression she could see from his lowered face. Then he looked up, meeting her gaze. "I didn't just leave the army because I'd served my time," he said. "I left on a forced medical discharge. My leg, the nightmares and, I'm guessing, the panic attacks since the storm, they are all results of the same thing."

Her mouth was dry, but she didn't want any more

wine. She needed a clear head for this, so she gulped water. "What thing?"

She had to know. Wouldn't rest until she knew.

And so badly didn't want to know that it was Greg it had happened to.

"The surprise attack that debilitated Duke." Stark words. Sent from white lips. She couldn't see him and not feel the horrid truth.

"You were there?"

"Not just there—I was directly in the line of fire. It should have been me who took the worst of it. He'd seen something, dived to a new position and got hit in midair. If not for that, my injuries would have been much worse." He didn't look away. Didn't miss a beat. But the moisture in his steady gaze, the puckering of his chin, the tight lips…they all spoke to her.

So loudly she could hardly think past the roaring in her ears.

Oh, God. Not Greg. Not Greg, too.

Her heart ached, but for him way more than for herself. The tears that sprang to her eyes were all for him. For the atrocities that stole soldiers' futures away from them in a blink.

"I lost a couple of brother comrades that day, too," he continued. "I'm the lucky one, Wendy." Reaching over, he brushed lightly against her cheek, removing the wetness there. "I wouldn't even have told you now, but…the nightmares…they aren't going to end. I didn't leave the other night because you aren't enough. I left because you are far too valuable for me to risk an unconscious middle-of-the-night attack."

She nodded. Had more to say. But he got there first.

"I want to adopt Jedi," he told her. "I need him, for so many reasons, but mostly so that someday, I can maybe spend the night at my parents' house again."

"And spend it other places, too?" Maybe with her. Maybe not. There was so much to think about.

"One day at a time," he told her. "But I won't be sleeping here until and unless I think it's safe, if that's what you mean. I'm not going to sit here and tell you that I don't want to have sex again, because it would be lying. I do. A whooole lot." His voice trembled as he drew out the one word. "But no way on earth will I be such a selfish ass as to ever put you in the position of having to open your heart to a lifetime of living with someone who suffers from the same disorder that took your brother…"

She wanted to tell him that the choice was hers to make, not his. But didn't speak. Because she feared that if she opened her mouth, she'd hear that her choice would be the same as the one he'd already made.

Some of the same internal demons that had killed her brother were living inside Greg, and he was right to be cautious about that, especially when it came to her.

And still, she had to point out… "That day you

were reading about nightmares...Jedi stopped the agitation that was coming on inside you."

Service dogs really helped. Using them as permanent treatment was valid, valuable, successful.

"I know. I need him. A confession I suspect you've been hoping all along you'd hear from me."

They were laying it all out there. "I knew he could help you, short term, at least. I was hoping that's all you'd need. You were refusing to see that you needed help." For a bare moment, she let herself be sad, because she was going to lose Jedi.

But then she focused on the joy, because she'd succeeded! Greg was going to take Jedi!

"I've come to realize that having to admit you're disappointed in yourself isn't a comfortable thing. I'm a guy. I'd grown fond of my emotional comfort."

If there had ever been a time to fall in love with Greg Martin, it would have been then. As it was, that moment...it would be with her forever.

"We'll take care of the paperwork tomorrow," she said aloud. Knowing, as she did so, that when he took Jedi home, there'd be no more reason for them to see each other so frequently.

They'd be back to the few times a month she needed him to fly for her.

And while she knew it was for the best, she also discovered that even a closed and guarded heart could break a little.

Chapter Nineteen

No. No. No. She was going downhill. He saw it, not only in the tears in her eyes but the drooping of her shoulders. The setness of her expression.

"I told you, earlier, I have a proposition for you…"

Blinking back tears, she nodded. "Right. The non-personal thing. I'd forgotten."

"I want us to go into business together," he blurted out instead of the speech that had been so carefully planned in his mind during the drive over.

Shaking her head, nose scrunched, she said, "You want to bring your investment group and my accounting firm into one entity? That makes no sense. Unless you're suggesting that we share clients, but even then…my clients are small-time, Greg. Very

few of them have enough funds left over for invest-
ing on a scale large enough to benefit you. And your
clients are way above my one-woman operation..."

He adored that scrunch in her nose. It was so cute
that it had no right to turn him on as much as it did.
But now was not the time to get distracted by his
arousal. He had a business proposal to pitch.

"I'm talking about matching pets with service animals, but doing it on a much larger scale. Like, na-
tionally. We'd be combining the concept behind Pets
for Vets with Pilots for Paws, but with nationwide
transportation capabilities. I'd spend more of the day-
to-day time running things, but we could have you
doing what you're already doing—scouring shelters
for viable service dogs and then bringing them into
our own training institute. Maybe even have veterans come to us to see which dog they bond with
most and vice versa..." Some of it was coming out
as planned. Words strung together as he'd practiced.
But not with any of the calm, the finesse, with which
he'd heard them in his mind earlier.

And when he saw the unmistakable glow that took
over her entire face, he just kept blabbing along. "I
can ask my dad to help us," he came up with out of
the blue. And knew he was on the perfect track there,
too. "He's got contacts all over the world. He could
be our communications liaison with the military."

He talked about finding travel contacts—a travel
agent, maybe—or just arranging case-by-case trans-

portation, depending on distance and time constraints.

"We could have a list of volunteers, including pilots, drivers, people willing to be companions to the animals on long train or bus rides…" Wendy said, and then stopped, as their gazes met once again. "It's a great idea, Greg."

"So you're in?"

"Yeah," she said and grinned. "I'm in."

His gut lightened. He took his first sip of wine. Felt, for the first time that day, as though he might actually enjoy his future life more than he would have being in the army. He might make himself proud.

But more… "Then, we'll be partners forever," he said softly. "In the way we can be."

She nodded, tearing up a little again, but smiling, too.

"Thank you."

"For what?"

"Finding a way to make us work."

He didn't want to fool her or himself. Neither of them could afford it. "I don't think I've done that, yet," he told her. "I've found a way to keep us together. Whether or not we can make it work remains to be seen."

Her expression serious again, she nodded. "There's the whole sex thing. We haven't really talked about it, but it's right here, gnawing at me."

"I know."

"You were the best I've ever had." He got so hard his zipper dug into him at that one.

"Ditto."

"It's not something we can just ignore."

"Agreed." He couldn't tear his gaze away from her. She seemed fairly glued to him, too, which pretty much made him her prisoner.

"You want to go to bed?"

"You have to ask?"

She grinned. "Good. I do, too"

"But I can't stay." And there was the crux. The damned cold shower on the heat of the moment.

"I know." Her gaze didn't falter. She didn't even blink.

"Are you good with that?"

"I understand it. I know it's not about me."

"Yeah, but are you good with it?"

Her shrug made sense to him. Who knew? This was uncharted territory for both of them.

"Hey, look at this way," she replied, with a bit of forced humor in her tone. "If we never live together, then when the hot sex wears off, we won't have to worry about someone moving out."

No, but… "What about when one or the other of us moves on?" At the moment, the thought of her with another man…

"Like you said, we're still looking for a way to make it work."

Right.

"My mother used to tell me not to borrow trouble," she offered then, and he wondered if that was before or after her mom had started drinking. Maybe someday he'd feel like he had the right to ask such a question.

Maybe someday he wouldn't think of questions like those.

Maybe, but he doubted it.

Because, with all of his self-honesty, he'd come to realize something else that had been growing on him. He didn't just want to have sex with Wendy Alvarez. Or go into business with her. He wanted to be her partner in life. To share her ups and downs. To be by her side when she was hurting, to bring her joy on Christmas morning. Maybe even to make babies with her.

He was head over heels in love with the woman.

He loved her so deeply that he'd rather die than risk exposing her to the darkness that lived hidden within him.

Wendy rode Greg as though it was the last ride she'd ever take. If she stopped, she'd have to get off, and…

He moved, igniting her, making her need for this the only reality, and she drove them both on until the explosion happened. Her eyes squeezed so tightly shut she saw stars. Her entire body felt the glorious waves pulsing inside her, all the way into her soul. Sex with Greg was that good, and she told herself that life didn't get any better than that.

Even after he left, taking Jedi with him, and when Goldie jumped up to lie at the end of her bed, Wendy was okay. Floating in lethargy and endorphins. Liking life just fine.

She lay there, letting the day slide over her. The revelations, the life-changing agreement she'd made to go into business with Greg…

It was all so…overwhelming.

And partly wonderful.

He'd seemed so sure his father would help.

She couldn't even imagine asking hers.

She couldn't help thinking of her family as it had been before Michael's time in the service, and afterward. Coupled with something Greg had said earlier that night.

Having to admit you're disappointed in yourself isn't a comfortable thing. He'd spent the past several years refusing to see who he'd become.

He hadn't been refusing to admit to *her* that he needed help, that he needed Jedi, he'd been refusing to admit it to himself.

And what about Michael? Had her brother seen himself as she'd seen him? Her memories were that of a fourteen-year-old girl. How could she possibly know?

What if Michael had seen himself differently than she'd seen him, the way that Greg had done? What if he'd seen the scarred, misshapen skin, been horrified by it, and thought he was horrifying her, too?

A memory surfaced. Her parents hadn't liked to

leave Michael alone, and that late afternoon duty of keeping him company had kind of tacitly fallen to Wendy. The fact that she'd come running straight home from school hadn't been at the behest of her parents. She'd just been that eager to get home to her big brother, thinking that he needed her.

Needing him to need her.

It was the only thing about the tragedy that had made sense to her. Michael finally needing her like she'd always needed him.

And when her mom had seen how much it meant to Wendy to tend to her brother, to spend that time with him, she'd started scheduling her own necessary errands during those hours, leaving brother and sister alone to have that time as just the two of them.

One day, Wendy had gotten out of school early and had come home to find her brother changing the bandage on the bad half of his face. She'd been so taken aback by the extent of the damage. It had hurt her to imagine the unbearable pain he had to have been suffering every time he chewed or talked. Just the thought of it had brought tears to her eyes. She must have sucked in air from the shock of it. He'd heard her, turned and screamed at her to get out and to never come back to his room without announcing herself first.

She'd refused to leave. Wanting to help him.

He'd been at his cantankerous worst, but after months of dealing with him, she was used to the verbal abuse. And when his face was rebandaged, when she brought him a chocolate milkshake half an hour later, he'd apologized. He'd said that he'd been trying to protect her from the ugliness.

She'd cried again, as she'd assured him that when she looked at him she didn't feel horror at the way he looked. She explained that her reaction was because she was imagining his pain.

But what if he hadn't been able to believe her?

What if the man he'd seen was so distasteful to himself that he couldn't conceive of any other way for others to view him?

He'd taken his life shortly after that.

And as she lay there in the darkness, she wondered, what if Michael hadn't killed himself because she hadn't done enough? What if it wasn't because her love hadn't been enough for him to hang on?

What if he'd been trying to spare her, or rather, spare any of his loved ones from the horror he'd surmised he'd become? Thinking others saw him as he'd seen himself?

Goldie lifted her head, resituated her body and laid her head back down on Wendy's foot. The weight felt good. Deep pressure therapy...

What if Michael's suicide hadn't been any reflection on her at all?

Had Michael, like Greg, been disappointed in himself? So much so that he'd been unable to go on?

She'd never know, of course. What-ifs were just

possibilities that hung around but weren't solid enough to hang your hat on.

And the rest… Her mother discovering in alcohol the oblivion she sought, and then sinking into it. Her father's affairs and absences. Her parents had lost a child. She couldn't imagine the devastation that had to have wrought. A pain that no one could be prepared to endure.

But they'd had another child, too. Another being of their own creation. One that was very much alive, right there trying to help, to grow up, to make them happy again. Make them proud. And the promise of her, the light that was her life, hadn't seemed to be even a candle in their darkness.

Her mom had lost Michael and her will to live.

And her dad had moved on to other people who could bring whatever he needed to his life. Whatever joy he found, whatever love, he hadn't been able to find it or share it with Wendy.

Her love hadn't been enough to salve his wound.

The story was the same as it had always been, brought her to the same place. She hadn't been enough to save her family. And yet…the story was different, too. Maybe, just maybe, the insights Greg had shared with her had given back to her a piece of the brother she'd lost. The only piece that, in the end, really mattered.

Perhaps Greg had given her back her belief in her brother's love. There was a chance Michael ended his life not because her love hadn't been enough but because his demons had just been too much for him to handle. Finally, she had an explanation that didn't diminish the love she'd been so certain she'd shared with her big brother.

So, yeah, life wasn't perfect. But that was why service was needed. And she knew she could find fulfillment in that, in serving those who were in need.

She could work to save the lives of soldiers like the one she'd loved and lost, to give another sister the gift of having her brother stay alive and heal.

She could be special friends with a wounded soldier and, with him, create a national organization that would give new life to thousands of veterans, instead of just hundreds. Could find loving, appreciative homes for thousands of rescue dogs who were as happy to serve as she was.

Her normal, happy, perfect world had imploded at fourteen. She'd ceased being a typical teenager the afternoon she'd come home to find her brother dead in front of his computer.

But she could still reach for the stars. Know moments of ecstasy. Contribute joy and hope to the world.

She could still be happy.

And so she would be.

Getting up long enough to pull on pajamas, she sent a quick text to Greg, saying good-night to him and Jedi, curled up on the bottom of her bed, cuddled up to Goldie and fell asleep.

* * *

Nowhere to run. To hide. People everywhere, soldiers down. One jolts. Flies backward. Another slumps forward. He has to stop it. Stop all of them. Fire. Explosions. Red-hot pain. Ignites fire within him.

He listens but can't hear for the screaming and sirens and explosions. Can't see. Too many flashes. Fire. Darkness.

It's up to him. Only him. His friend is down—Duke needs him. He has to fight his way out. Their way out.

Gun in hand gets knocked away. His finger hits the trigger as it goes. Gunfire. But they won't get him. Won't win. Won't take everyone from him.

He swings. Swings again. Hitting air and...

Hearing a bark?

Dying of heat, of the pain in his leg, Greg swung his head, looking for a dog in the rubbish, and saw one. Sitting at the side of his bed, peering over the mattress at him.

Jedi.

A dog he knew.

Head moving slowly, eyes peering, he glanced around him. Recognized the dresser. The doorway. The walls.

His home.

He was dripping with sweat. Reached for a tissue from his nightstand and saw the phone sitting there. Had Wendy ever answered his text? He'd fallen asleep waiting...

Wendy. She'd texted good-night.

He'd replied—with a question she hadn't answered. Not yet, anyway.

Jedi was right there, staring at him.

Another nightmare. Not surprising, considering all of the lives he'd lived the day before. The memories. The heightened emotions.

His unanswered text.

And Jedi.

The dog's bark had woken him. Jedi was safe.

But Greg had swung. He'd hit nothing but air.

If Wendy had been in bed with him, he'd have hit her.

If Jedi had been in bed with him…

The reading he'd been doing on nightmares the day Jedi had nudged him out in the yard had said that in order for a service dog to be most effective against nightmares, he had to sleep in the bed with his owner. It was the only way for the dog to sense the symptoms in time to wake his owner before the nightmare got in full swing.

Jedi had known but not soon enough to stop the nightmare from blossoming in his mind.

He'd woken him.

Too late.

But what if he'd allowed the dog on his bed?

When he'd first climbed into bed, Jedi had jumped up and lain down. Greg, afraid he'd hurt the dog unknowingly, had ordered him off.

Rightfully protecting the dog? Or stubbornly refusing help?

He grabbed his phone. Set his fingerprint to unlock it. And saw the text screen he'd left open.

His own message, Are we making a mistake here?

Still with no response.

His leaving Wendy to come home and sleep alone hadn't been a mistake. He'd known that with certainty even before the nightmare. But Wendy being left? That felt wrong.

When he'd done it, he'd known she deserved more.

When he'd sent the text, he'd been ready to tell her that, too.

And lying there after the nightmare, he still knew it. He sucked in air. Tried to even his breathing—always the first step of recovery.

Called Jedi up. Praised the young dog. Pet him. Watched the sun start to rise.

And heard his phone ding with an incoming text.

Dreading the answer that might be awaiting, he took a couple of seconds before looking. Jedi, eyes closed, gave a long sigh.

After having his night's sleep interrupted, the German shepherd deserved his rest.

His hand still running lazily alone the dog's back, Greg lifted his phone.

Read.

Having second thoughts about the business?

Damn. Jedi glanced up when Greg pulled his hand swiftly from the dog's fur. Of course not, he typed as fast as he could.

Then, what?

You. There alone. You deserve better. More.

I'm not alone. Goldie's here.

Oddly enough, he got that. Jedi's here.

Good.

He meant to reply. Was considering what to say next, discarded all of the sexy or emotional responses that came to mind and woke up an hour later with his phone still in his hand, Jedi snoring beside him.

Once upon a time, he'd wanted a wife. Kids.

What his parents had.

But that wasn't his life. It was theirs.

So he loved a woman he couldn't marry. It wasn't ideal, but he could still be the best friend she ever had. And maybe someday, if he had ample proof that Jedi could catch nightmare symptoms in time, he'd even agree to spend all night in her arms once in a while.

Or, better yet, he'd be a good enough friend to be able to help her find a way to open her heart to a man who could spend every night in her bed, holding her in his arms, letting her feel how very much she was loved.

Even as he had the thought, he knew that was what he had to do. During his time with Wendy, he had to help her let down her walls so she could let in the man that had to be out there, waiting to give her the love she'd been seeking since she was fourteen years old.

And on his side, if he could be a man who could give up the love of his life so that she could be her happiest self—then, he would finally be a guy he could be proud of. He could live with being the man who was strong enough to love a woman so much he'd willingly put her happiness above his own.

It was time to be that man.

To live his best life.

Chapter Twenty

Greg's father was eagerly on board with their new nonprofit business. Greg would serve as executive director for the time being. He'd get the paperwork done and file what had to be provided to the government. Randolph was already putting out feelers with the military to get the necessary contacts lined up. And Wendy had started a much broader list of shelters who'd notify her anytime they might have a dog come in that fit her basic requirements.

A little over a week after Greg had first suggested that they go into business together, Wendy was sitting at her desk in town after her last appointment, Goldie on the floor beside her while she sent out emails to shelters all over the country. She needed to get it all done before she had to head off for her dinner plans.

Greg's parents had driven up to his place for a couple of days—a downside of which was he hadn't been to Wendy's. But tonight, the three Martins were coming into Spring Forest to have dinner with Wendy at Veniero's, the elder Martins' treat. They wanted to meet their son's business partner and discuss the national venture in person.

The upscale Italian restaurant was new to town, and though she'd heard wonderful things about its excellent and authentic southern Italian dishes, that Thursday night would be the first time she'd ever eaten there. Had she and Greg been an item, she might have been more nervous, but since they were just business partners with fringe benefits that no one knew about, she was kind of looking forward to the evening—curious to meet the couple who'd borne and raised Greg.

Her nerves came to life the second Greg walked into the restaurant and saw her standing there, waiting for them. Due to the dressiness of the place, she'd worn a red, figure-hugging Lycra and cotton dress to work that day, and with the way he was looking at her, she might as well have been naked. The heat in his eyes matched what she was feeling as she took in the sight of him. His long legs and broad shoulders in a suit didn't do a thing to calm her.

"You ever do it in a public restroom?" Greg whispered to her as they followed his parents to the table his father had reserved.

Even more heat shot through her body, landing simultaneously in her face…and her crotch. She was only able to partially pull herself together by the time his mother, in a stylish sleeveless cotton black-and-white dress, turned to direct Wendy to the seat next to Greg, directly across from his father. Like they were a family. Realizing how they must look to the other diners around them, she quickly sat and hid her tightly clenched hands in her lap beneath the white tablecloth, thankful for the candlelight that cast shadows on everyone.

Greg's knee nudged hers. She nudged him back, not gently. Conversation continued. Greg's mother chattered much of the time. Wanting to know what everyone was going to eat. Analyzing the menu. Asking Wendy how long she'd lived in Spring Forest and where her office was located. Meanwhile, Greg and his father sat, mostly silent. And Greg's knee seemed to develop a twitch that kept it in touch with hers much of the time.

After dinner they talked about the new nonprofit, and Wendy was gratified, and also a bit shocked, to hear how much work Randolph had already done, what he was proposing to take on and the reading he'd done on both veterans in need of service dogs and dog training as well to prepare himself for the work. The man rarely spoke but managed to express a whole lot.

He reminded her of Greg in many ways. In just that quick hour she saw a connection between father and son, a deep respect that ran equally between them, a bond that she'd never seen between Michael and her dad. Randolph didn't hover; he didn't try to take over their business or have a say in major decisions. He deferred to Wendy and Greg on every issue he raised. But he gave them the benefit of his astuteness and his backing and was clearly eager to put action behind that support.

Maybe if Michael had had some of that same male familial guidance... Not that she blamed her father for her brother's death, but maybe, if Steve Alvarez had been more aware of others' needs...

Was it wrong to envy her friend his intact and emotionally invested family?

Greg's parents excused themselves to the restroom while they waited for after-dinner coffees, and when Greg leaned toward her, she braced herself for a sexual barrage. Was eager for the distraction. And the connection.

"What's wrong?" he asked instead.

Did he have to see everything? Wanting to give him a nonchalant *Nothing*, she heard herself say, "Watching you with your parents, hearing you all talk about your sisters—the way your dad sits there quietly but is like the glue that binds your book— it makes me think that what I thought was a perfect family before my brother got injured probably wasn't. What you all have, it would have weathered

Michael's injuries. And might even have been strong enough to handle his demons…"

"You don't know that."

He was right. She didn't. But it made sense to her in a way nothing had in a very long time. Maybe Greg wasn't the only one who'd been carrying around false images of himself.

As they were waiting for the bill, the talk turned to Goldie, who was still at Wendy's office. Greg's mom, Dianne, asked after her, admitting that she'd heard about the dog from Birdie and Bunny that afternoon when she'd visited with the sisters. Wendy had told Bethany about her newest houseguest when she'd stopped in to arrange for Jedi's permanent adoption, and it seemed that Bethany had shared the news with the Whitaker sisters.

"I've been bringing her to work every day," Wendy said. "She's used to being with her owner 24-7, and I don't want to leave her alone too much."

"You're planning to keep her, then?" After an hour in the woman's company, Wendy found Dianne's questions more of a compliment than an intrusion. Greg's mother clearly looked after those in her sphere. Besides, it was nice to have someone so interested in learning everything about her.

She shook her head immediately. She'd thought about getting a dog, but having lost Jedi…she just didn't think she was ready. Besides… "She'll be happier working," Wendy stated the deciding factor, not the other elements that had also contributed to her

decision. "I've been looking all week and was thinking—" she looked at Randolph "—that maybe you'd
know someone…"

She glanced at Greg, who was studying her with
some intent, and switched her attention immediately
back to his father. Randolph said he'd be on the watch
for someone who'd need the dog as much as the dog
needed a home.

"Randolph and I…we're both huge believers in
what you're doing," Dianne said then, wearing a
smile that seemed to encompass the entire table.
"Having met Jedi, we can see what a gift a dog like
that would be."

"Speaking of which," Randolph said, "how did
things go with Duke yesterday?"

"Same as always," Greg shrugged, but then
grinned. "He moved his fingers on Jedi, though.
Three weeks in a row now."

Wendy had already heard the news through text
message the day before. And…it hit her.

"Wait," she blurted out so loudly people at the next
table glanced over. For a place that exuded elegance,
she'd been a bit brass. She didn't even care. "You
said Duke's sister—Julie, I think?—lives alone…"

"That's right," Greg confirmed.

"Is she a dog person?" Wendy asked excitedly.

Greg, still looking bewildered, nodded. "I know
they had one growing up. And she took in Duke's
collie when he left for the service. Chappy died more
than five years ago, but—"

"Goldie!" Wendy said, with a glance toward the elder Martins again. "You said Julie visits Duke every evening. If she brought Goldie with her, then the dog would get her service time but not have to be on the job 24-7 anymore, which would be better for her at her age. And Duke...right now he gets Jedi once a week, but what if he had a dog every single day?" She paused, briefly, as her heart contracted at the thought of losing the companion who'd been sharing her bed for over a week, but she pushed forward. "And Julie would have a housemate trained to pay attention to her, to give her back some of the caring she gives so faithfully to her brother." Just the thought of giving a veteran's sister a piece of love and loyalty while she served her brother... It made Wendy's world right. And if, by some miracle, Goldie could help Duke...

"I think it's a great idea!" Dianne's voice filled the void where Greg's should have been.

After a couple of seconds, her son said, "I'll give Julie a call, if you'd like..."

Wendy heard the hesitation in Greg's voice, but her nod, her smile...she couldn't contain them. She understood what it was to be a sister to an injured veteran. She knew how hard it was to see him suffer. Knew the need to be by his side every day.

Maybe it wouldn't happen. Maybe Julie wouldn't want a dog. And Wendy would get to keep Goldie a while longer.

But despite her sadness at the thought of saying

goodbye to the animal, she was full of joy and excitement at the idea that she'd be able to help someone else who'd also lost the brother she'd known. It felt like she'd come full circle. Was a part of the circle.

For that little piece of time, it felt like Greg's family was a part of the circle, too. Like she was a part of them.

And that made it a happy moment.

After a couple of nights without sex with Wendy, Greg made it to three orgasms Friday night. Their lives were moment to moment, and he was going to make those moments the absolute best they could be. He slid off of her that last time with deep regret but also satiated in ways that went far beyond the physical.

"You could stay." Her words weren't a question. Nor were they a command. They weren't even a suggestion, really. Just an audible declaration of what would always be there, hanging in the air between them. "You've got Jedi."

Now, that was more in the way of persuasion, and he couldn't fall prey to that.

He wanted to. God, how he wanted to!

"And you have to be back in the morning, anyway…"

They were taking Goldie to Julie in the morning. Meeting Duke's sister in Duke's room, actually, as she was spending a good part of the day there to watch a baseball doubleheader with her brother and

Wendy thought that would be a great time to introduce Goldie to her new people. It would give the three of them a chance to spend their first hours as a family bonding all together.

He sat up. "We can't keep doing this if we can't accept it for what it is," he said, his heart heavy.

She didn't want to be left. He got it. And knew that she needed to be with someone who could give her what she needed. What she deserved.

They both knew that couldn't be him.

He was just one more continuous leaver, strengthening her sense that being left was normal...

Wendy scooted up beside him, propped on a pillow, their naked bodies a foot apart as she held the covers to her chest.

As though he didn't know every single inch of those breasts...their feel, their taste, their scent.

But probably a good call to take away temptation.

His job was to help her open her heart enough to let in the man who was meant for her. He'd been doing a pretty damned bad job at it.

Sure, he could have sex with her until the other guy showed up, but his leaving every time was entirely counterproductive to the end goal.

Him loving and leaving was another nail on the boards around her heart every single time.

"You could sleep on the couch." Her words came softly, but not tentatively. "Just for tonight, not as a way of life," she quickly amended before he even had a chance to glance her way.

He didn't look, though he'd been about to. Instead, he tried to sit there naked with her and weigh the pros and cons of her suggestion against the ultimate objective.

"Do you ever sleepwalk when you have nightmares?" she asked.

He nodded, still back on her previous statement. And then he answered, "Not in a while," when he caught up to where she was going with the question.

"I could lock this door, if that would make you feel better. And…you have Jedi."

He knew what she was doing. But he had to think about what *he* was doing. More to the point, what he didn't seem to be doing well. He was holding on to her, which was the last thing she needed.

The other night with his parents, she'd seemed to settle right into being a daughter figure, treating them like parents—not her own, but the parents of a friend. There was something in the note of her voice, the way she'd looked at them…he couldn't really place it. Maybe it boiled down to respect.

He was getting off track. Letting her confuse him.

If he stayed once, she'd want him to stay again. And before you knew it, he'd be bringing things to leave in her house. Having her bring things to his home to leave in his spare room.

One of the six of them.

How did being in the moment start so clean and get so messy so quickly?

"Has Jedi been sleeping on the bed with you?"

"Yeah."

"Have you had any more nightmares?"

"I'm not sure."

She nudged his shoulder, and he finally glanced her way. "How can you not be sure?" she asked, their faces so close he could see the lightest green glints dotting her eyes.

"He woke me once. I don't remember a nightmare, but it could have been starting…" He couldn't get his hopes up. There were no miracle cures. "He could also just have been stretching or scratching an itch."

"How did he wake you?"

She knew too much. "He whined," Greg admitted. Service dogs were trained to whine when they perceived nightmares and to keep their distance from a sleeping owner. "But you know how he gives that whine when he's scratching sometimes. And his stretching sigh sounds a lot like a whine."

All true. And necessary for them to keep in mind.

"Your parents stayed with you…"

And suddenly things started to make sense. She thought that since they'd stayed in the same house—maybe because of Jedi's introduction to his life—that the circumstances were changing. "They stay in a guest wing. It has its own outside entrance with a dead-bolt lock on the door connecting to the rest of the residence."

He waited for more—and he felt deflated, in spite of himself, when it didn't come. It felt like she'd run out of chances for him.

That was his cue to move in with his own responsibilities. "Do you want kids?"

The question was too personal for their in-the-moment coupling, and he knew it probably sounded abrupt and out of nowhere to her. He just didn't know any other way to get her to reach for more than what she had.

"It's not a likely possibility for me."

"That's not what I asked."

"*I* don't ask, Greg." Her emphasis was clear.

"Maybe you should."

"Why? It's like wanting to have wings because it would be cool to be able to fly…"

"Not really." He knew he was pushing, but he couldn't stop. "If you don't ask, you limit who you can be, what you can become." Her wing comment hit so close to home, he knew he was doing the right thing. He'd asked himself years before when the only life he'd ever envisioned had been taken from him. He'd been trying to picture what could possibly come next, and the only thing that had sounded at all fulfilling to him had been a life in the sky. He'd wanted to fly. He hadn't had wings. But he'd bought some…

"What's the point here?" Her voice was growing querulous.

The point was to get her to ask herself for more. To help her fight for what she wanted or needed. To fight for her greatest happiness.

"It was a simple enough question. Could you be a good mother? Do you want that for your life?"

"Of course." Sounding affronted, she shot the answer out with no hesitation.

And he knew he'd just taken the first step toward losing her to a man who could give her everything she needed.

Chapter Twenty-One

Greg didn't stay. After the whole pregnancy discussion, she was kind of relieved to have him gone. To have her space comfortably and securely to herself again.

Taking a long hot shower, she let the troubles of the world wash off her. She gave up the worry and fear and heartache, too, for the time she stood there and just reveled in the relaxing, physical pleasure. Even humming for a second or two.

She liked being alone. Liked the control she had of her world when she was alone.

Then she got out of the shower. Saw Goldie lying in the middle of the bathroom floor, waiting for her, and started to cry.

She'd only had the Lab for a short time, but she was going to miss her, that was for sure.

She was also incredibly excited at the thought of Julie and Duke gaining the Lab as a family member. They had real joy coming their way, and that far, far outweighed her small bit of sadness.

At least, her sadness over losing Goldie. Her sadness over Greg, on the other hand, felt like it might just be beginning. Because while they'd agreed to continue what they had, he seemed to be looking for any excuse to pull away.

If she got pregnant somehow, would she keep the child?

Would she be a good mother?

Of course.

That didn't mean she wanted kids.

She didn't.

Hadn't even thought about it until Greg practically forced the question into her mind.

She wasn't going to turn up pregnant. She and Greg used condoms. Carefully. Every single time.

But…had she ever thought she wanted kids?

Maybe, as a pubescent teen, right after her cycle had started.

Before Michael came home.

How did you think about having children when you had no family to bring them into?

In flannel pants and a cutoff T-shirt she wandered around her rented home—rented so there'd be no worry about getting so attached that her soul got ripped if she lost it—and pushed back at the questions Greg had raised. What was he after? What answers had he expected from her? Did he want to rub it in that even if she'd be a good mother, she'd be raising the child entirely on her own?

She didn't have a Randolph and Dianne and irritating sisters to love a kid to death.

The only family she had left to give a kid was her dad.

In her living room, pulling her bare feet onto the couch with her—her own couch, albeit second hand—she dialed her father's cell. Wherever he was, it wasn't in the States, so it was likely that it was not the middle of the night. She'd listen to his voice on his voice mail. Leave a message.

He wouldn't call back anytime soon.

But he'd acknowledge that she'd called when he finally did.

Or he'd text.

"Hello?"

Wendy gulped, started curling her fingers around her toes like she used to do sitting on the floor waiting to open presents on Christmas morning. "Papa?"

"*Hija mia*! Everything okay?"

"Yep. Fine! I'm starting a new business."

"That's nice! I'm sure you'll do well at it. How's your weather there?"

"Good. Warm." Dark, moonless, but the sun was supposed to be up in the morning… "How about there?"

"Sunny."

That was it. No details.

"Where are you?"

"Heading toward the UK," he said, sounding as though something else had just grabbed his attention. "We're supposed to be docking later this afternoon."

United Kingdom. Not even a specific country. Seemed like a world away.

"So, if everything's okay, I should probably..."

"You ever wish you had grandchildren, Papa?" she interrupted his sign-off, holding her breath, even as she knew that she was just setting herself up for disappointment. It was incredibly unlikely that he'd give her the answer she actually wanted to hear.

"Nah," he told her, just as she'd figured he would. "You aren't pregnant, are you?" She suddenly seemed to have his full attention.

"Would it bother you if I was?"

"Of course not! You're a grown woman."

"Would you *like* it if I was? If I got pregnant some-how, would you want me to keep the child?"

"If it's what you wanted."

Would you be a good grandpapa? The question hung there. She didn't ask it. To do so would be un-fair. Her dad was who he was.

He didn't get that he wasn't who she needed him to be.

Or if he did, he didn't seem able or willing to change that.

"I love you, Papa."

"Love you, too, *Princesa*…"
And that was that.

Greg should have known that it didn't bode well that Wendy came out of her house with a forty-ounce-sized travel mug of coffee Saturday morning. As previously arranged, he'd brought Jedi to stay at her house while they transported Goldie to Duke's, as the dog seemed much more comfortable alone in the smaller space. Greg had yet to leave the pup alone at his place.

She didn't offer Greg any coffee, just helped Goldie up into the back seat of his SUV, climbed into the front passenger seat, buckled herself in and sipped at her mug. In capri pants and a Furever Paws short-sleeved T-shirt, her hair neatly braided and bangs straight, she looked lovely and put together, and yet she somehow still seemed…off.

"Rough night?"

"Nope." Her tone expressly discouraged further questioning on the matter.

Okay, then. She wasn't in a talking mood. He'd hoped to discuss some new ideas he'd come up with for the business, but if she wanted silence, he would comply.

Five miles down the road, when she finally did start to speak, he wished they'd stuck to silence.

"You want kids, Greg?"

Greg, not the sassy *Martin* she usually used when she addressed him.

"I couldn't be a good father to little ones. Not in my condition."

"That's not what I asked. I asked if you want them."

"I don't think about it."

"Exactly."

Wow. He'd really pissed her off with his questions the previous night. He wished he could be sure that was a good thing.

"You sure you want to give up Goldie?" he asked then, thinking maybe her tension was escalated due to the morning's errand. "There's still time to change your mind…"

"Julie's expecting Goldie." Interesting response—most definitely not an answer to his question.

"She hasn't met Goldie, yet. We can find her another dog. It's the overall idea that I'm happy about—a dog for Julie. I'd been playing with the idea of a dog for Duke, trying to figure out how that would work, but your solution is much better. Still, there's no reason why it has to be Goldie."

"She's expecting a dog this morning. We can't find another one by then. And I want her to have Goldie. It feels like the right match. For both of them."

"But you're going to miss her."

"I miss Jedi, too. And other dogs I've worked with at the shelter. It's all part of the business."

Right. Their business.

He started talking to her about his ideas. Starting with letting him pony up enough seed money to hire a work-from-home admin to handle phone calls and basic paperwork, set up databases, that kind of thing. They'd already talked about writing grants for funding, but that would take some time.

She liked the idea, and they spent the rest of the drive making plans.

Once at the private nursing facility where Duke lived, she was all business, getting Goldie down, talking calmly and reassuring her, and grabbing the folder of paperwork necessary for the Lab's adoption.

Greg almost nixed the whole plan when, outside Duke's door, Wendy paused. Petting Goldie's head, she went down on her haunches to speak softly in Goldie's ear, giving her a brief hug and kissing her on the bridge of her nose. Greg couldn't catch most of what he said, but he heard *Thank you* loud and clear.

Wendy needed Goldie. Just as he needed Jedi.

She'd helped him. Why couldn't he help her?

He was still asking the question when she pushed open the ajar door to Duke's room and led Goldie inside.

Julie was already on her feet, approaching the pair, when Greg got his first glimpse into the room. From there, he stood back. The two sisters to fallen veterans introduced themselves, and as they did so, their eyes grew moist, and a bubble seemed to form around them, taking them into a world where they were related, leaving him out to go greet his friend as though it were any other day.

And after all of the official passing of information

from Wendy to Julie regarding Goldie took place, that was it. Wendy was ready to go.

She'd done what she'd come to do.

Had already said her goodbyes.

Goldie had ceased being hers the minute she'd walked in that door.

He got it all, just watching it happen. Reminded himself that she'd delivered many, many dogs to families who needed them over the years he'd known her. And planned to deliver a lifetime more.

But Goldie had been hers. Only for days, but from what he knew, that old Lab had been the only dog Wendy had ever had as her own since she was a kid.

Her giving Goldie away…bothered him.

A lot.

More than a lot.

It was as though giving that dog away was burning out the last hope that she'd ever be able to keep someone she loved in her life.

Maybe that hope had already burned, long ago.

She made it back outside, climbed in his SUV without a word. He glanced her way as he started the vehicle, took stock of her calm demeanor. The lack of tears, or any sign of emotion, bothered him.

"It's all right to cry, you know."

"Is there something wrong with not crying?" The question clearly wasn't issued with an expectation of response.

"It's not healthy to keep everything bottled up inside."

"Like you're one to talk?"

"Just saying…"

He hated feeling inept. Without clear direction.

She'd probably push him away if he offered a hug. What could he offer that would help and that she'd accept? The mood was all wrong for sex—

The realization made him sad.

"You want to stop having sex with me?"

That got her attention, and her face turned sharply toward him. "Did I say I did?"

"No."

He waited. Then asked, "But do you?" He needed to know where they stood. Touching each other intimately required an understanding of boundaries, or lack of them, that had to be clearly spoken.

Five minutes passed. He waited but wasn't going to let it go.

"No, I don't want that to end." Wendy's words, softly given, went straight to his heart. Filling him with relief.

And confusion.

"What do you want?" he finally asked.

He was done guessing. Tired of doubting himself.

"I want my perfect family back. Except that, when I look back now, I'm not sure I ever had it at all."

"You wouldn't have felt so loved for fourteen years if there hadn't been real love there." There was no doubt in his mind about that one.

"I guess."

He wasn't helping.

"Do *you* want to stop the sex?" she asked a few moments later. "Is that why you asked? Is it getting too messy for you?"

"No."

She didn't turn to him, but he saw the smile break out on her face, and he smiled, too.

Lord knew where in the hell they were going to end up, what mistakes they'd end up paying for, but one thing was for sure: there was still a connection between them. And as messy as it might get, he wasn't willing to let that go.

Chapter Twenty-Two

He'd finally asked a question she could answer. She wanted him in her bed, on top of her, giving her moments of feeling fully alive.

And he'd told her what she'd needed to hear.

He wanted it, too.

"We don't have to solve the world in a day," she said as he pulled off the highway into Spring Forest.

"It would be cool if we could." His response relaxed her.

"You want to come over for dinner tonight?" she asked.

He looked her way. A look that told her he was hungry for a lot more than food, and she smiled. They were okay.

Everything would be fine.

"How about you come to my place?" The thought struck fear in her. His place…his things…his space… she'd get in too deep.

Want things she couldn't have.

Want things she didn't want to want.

"I have to work today." It wasn't even noon yet.

He pulled up in front of her house.

"Why do I think you're making an excuse not to come to Hendrix?" he asked shrewdly.

His town. But from what she'd heard, his place was outside town—encompassing many acres of wooded privacy. It sounded amazing. What if she never wanted to leave?

Why did she constantly seem to want what she couldn't have? Even if she broke all of her own rules, changed who she wanted to be in her new life…he couldn't offer her a perfect home. Or any home.

"Maybe because I am."

But…what if he felt the same way about coming to her house? "Would you rather not come into Spring Forest?" They could see if there was a motel half- way in between where they could meet.

She didn't really like the idea—at all—but maybe it would suit them better all around. Less intimate. Less chance of fooling themselves into thinking the sex was more than simply that.

"I like being here." He was looking at her. She had to turn her head and look back at him.

"You do?"

His gaze held hers solidly as he said, "I do."

And she could breathe again.

Greg took Jedi up for a flight over the ocean, thought about a day when maybe Wendy could be sitting in the dog's place with him. Even if that meant there was someone else in the back seat with her. He wanted to show her the dolphins.

He timed his landing well enough to catch a rideshare to his favorite fresh-seafood market and pick up some salmon. Jedi, vest on, was at attention beside him the entire time.

With the shopping done, the two of them headed back to the plane, landed at home, and took his vehicle to Spring Forest. A quick ride through town showed him that Wendy was still at the office with clients, and he took Jedi to her place for his feeding and medication. And then to make the baked salmon and red potatoes that were his favorite of his mother's recipes.

Dinner was ready when she walked in the door, wine poured so that he could hand her a glass in greeting.

"I didn't want the house to be empty your first night with Goldie gone," he said.

She smiled. He almost leaned in for a kiss.

What in the hell was he doing?

Jedi nudged her hand, and she bent down to kiss the bridge of his nose.

He was being a friend, Greg reminded himself. Helping her through a rough day.

Maybe trying to show her what it would be like if she'd open her heart to someone capable of filling her life full-time.

The guy could even be out there already, in her life, ready for her, just waiting for her to be ready for him.

She ate as much salmon as he did. What he'd pegged as leftovers for her lunch wasn't left over. They spent an hour going over new business items, and it felt damned good, sitting there with her, his tablet and her laptop open, with pens and yellow pads filled with notes in front of both of them.

And when they were through, they headed down the hallway to her bed as naturally as if they'd been doing so all of their lives.

After they'd shared the first climax, while he was still inside her, she looked up at him, her gaze completely serious. His heart stopped for a second. And she said, "You asked me if I wanted to stop having sex with you," she said softly, almost hoarsely. "These moments with you, our time out of time—they're probably selfish. If you need to slow down, I'm good with that. But…these moments…" Looking up at him, she said, "They're the best moments in my life, Greg. These are the moments when I fly."

Her eyes were moist again.

And he had to blink, to swallow hard, before he could say, "Me, too."

They didn't talk after that. Not with words. But their bodies spent the next couple of hours giving each other the things they couldn't ask for, the things they couldn't talk about.

The things that, in real life, they'd never have together.

She was ready that night, when Greg had to pull away from her and go. She got up when he did. Pulled on her robe as he dressed in the jeans and pullover he'd had on when he'd shown up at her door that morning.

Only, after he was dressed, he didn't call Jedi, walk down the hall to the front door and leave. He called his dog. Walked down the hall. And stopped in the living room to turn and look at her.

"I can't give you the things you want most," he said. "I can be the best business partner you'll ever have and a great friend, but I can't be the missing figure in your perfect family."

The words, coming after the lovemaking they'd just shared, felt like a slap. She knew their truth. Was standing there watching him go because she knew.

But for him…

"The thing is, Wen," he continued, "I think that there's a man out there who can give you those things."

She wanted to shake her head. Was too numb to do anything.

"I know you think you aren't enough. I even get

why you think it. But being with you—watching you with everyone who comes in contact with you, canine or human—you've got the biggest giving capacity of anyone I've ever known."

Her bottom lip trembled, but she wouldn't cry. She knew what being left felt like. Knew how to get through it.

"The thing is…your family went through a horrible tragedy. Your dad…maybe he's just not capable of loving as deeply as you do. But that doesn't mean that there aren't a lot of people out there who are capable. Who do care. Who would stay if you'd give them the chance."

For a second there, she thought he was talking about himself. In that one brief flash, her heart started to crack. And then he said, "I'm safe, because you know I can't be that man. But you can be that woman for someone else, Wen. You are enough and then some."

Tears seeped through that small new crack in her heart. She didn't let them fall. "How would you know?"

"Goldie would have stayed."

He was talking about an abandoned service dog she'd had for less than a month. So how could his words hit her so profoundly?

So painfully?

She'd given sweet Goldie a family that would love her until death. That was a good thing.

"Maybe it's not so much that you aren't enough

to compel people to stay but that you aren't giving anyone a chance to convince you to let them in. Not even a dog."

She heard her sudden intake of breath more than she felt it. Stared at him. Lost.

"That was a little harsh, don't you think?"

"Yes," he agreed. But he didn't take it back.

"What I'm saying is that you don't have to settle for moments out of time, sweetie. You don't have to settle for living the rest of your life sleeping alone in your bed. The second you open your heart up, shine your green light, forever love is going to find you. You're one in a million, and your shine is too brilliant to miss."

He turned away and let himself out.

Missing the stream of tears falling down her cheeks.

For the second night in a row, Wendy didn't get much rest. And that very long Saturday night, she didn't have Goldie by her side, either.

It was the first night in weeks that she was the only living being in her home. The only one breathing the air.

She sputtered. Grumbled some. Cleaned.

She cried.

Ate some chocolate ice cream, dumped most of the scoop she'd served herself down the sink. Took a hot bath.

And somewhere between midnight and dawn, she

looked herself in the mirror, hair down, sweaty from her bath and all aflutter. She stared into her weepy green eyes and knew.

Greg was right.

She'd been so busy trying to fix him, the same way that she tried to fix everyone. All those years, she'd thought she'd been helping members of a walk of life she'd escaped: the walking wounded. She hadn't seen that, all along, she'd been one of them, too.

Michael's battle scars might not have been on her body, but they'd seared her heart as surely as if they had been. And she'd let that heart wither beneath the burns.

She was alive, but not living.

She loved parts of her life. Loved Spring Forest. Helping her clients. Most of all she loved the work she did with service dogs and the veterans who needed them—work that Greg was growing with her in ways she'd never even dared dream about.

Maybe she'd even be able to sell her accounting business at some point, if they could get to the point where their nonprofit was self-supporting enough to allow her to draw enough of a salary to pay her bills.

Her eyes looked back from the mirror.

She was doing it again. Thinking about the giving, the serving, to avoid letting her own heart be personally exposed.

Back to the wall, she slid down to her bathroom floor. Started to shake.

Tears fell in a cascade until she felt like a puddle on the floor.

And asked herself what she really wanted.

Looked inside to see who was really there.

Who she could be.

She searched for her joy.

It took hours. Eventually she wandered into the living room. Fell to the couch. Dawn came and went. Maybe she dozed some, she couldn't be sure. But by feeding time at Furever Paws, Wendy was dressed in shorts and a cotton top, clothes that felt good, not ones behind which she could hide, and was waiting for Bethany to appear.

She stated her intentions, signed necessary paperwork and walked out.

Got in her SUV. Typed an address into the satnav.

And followed the GPS instructions without ever looking back.

Greg had been up for hours, was just coming out of the gym, Jedi at his side, when he caught sight of the security-camera screen sitting on his kitchen counter. A vehicle had entered his property and was on the way down his drive.

A familiar vehicle.

Wendy?

"Come on, Jedi," he said, pulling the towel from his neck to wipe his face and shoulders as he headed out the front door.

Something had to be wrong, horribly wrong, for

Wendy to be arriving at his place at all, let alone before ten on a Sunday morning, after the way they had left things.

He was standing at the circular drive in front of his place when she stopped. Waited on the sidewalk as she came to him, taking stock of every inch of her.

She was different.

Vastly different.

He hardly recognized her.

But couldn't...

"Your hair's down." He'd kissed every inch of her body, been inside her many times in many ways and he'd never seen her hair free of its braid.

And she was wearing shorts...and a tank top. Wearing her natural beauty, rather than playing it down.

Like she'd been set free.

And was coming to set him free? To tell him that she was going to take his advice and give life a chance?

She handed him a piece of paper.

"What's this?"

Her resignation from a business they hadn't even officially registered?

"Open it."

He did. And read.

She'd adopted a puppy.

"She's one of the ones from the backyard breeder litters. She's not spayed yet or ready to come home, but when she's ready, she's mine."

He grinned, so proud of her he couldn't contain himself from reaching out and giving her a hug, rubbing his beard against her neck to tickle her.

A friend connection, not a sexual one.

When he let go, she stood there nose to nose with him, shoulders back, and said, "I know what I want, Greg."

He'd figured it was coming. Told himself he was ready for her to say that she was ending things with him, setting her sights on a real relationship with someone who could give her a real commitment.

"You were right. What you said last night about me being closed off to forever love. And that bit about babies the other night. I do want them. I want a husband. I want a family. My own family."

He needed to hug her again. To hide the slight trembling in his smiling lips. He'd never known it could be possible for a heart to truly soar and to wither a little at the same time.

"After dinner with your folks, seeing you with them, the way they're helping with the business, the way they've been there for you…it's so different from what I saw in my own family. But it's what I want. And you know why I want it?"

He shook his head.

"Because the bond you guys share is what sees you through the tough times. You don't quit. You find a way to roll with it. Roll through it. That's what I want."

"Then, you will have it." There was no doubt in

his mind, or his heart. He could feel his eyes moist-
ening, not with full-blown tears but with an emotion
he didn't even recognize.

He loved her so much.

Was so relieved that she was going to be truly
happy.

"But the thing is, I know for certain there is no
other man out there, waiting to give it all to me."

What now?

Surely she wasn't going to throw another wrench
into her possibility for happiness.

"You want to know how I know?" she asked.

He wasn't sure he did. "I guess."

"Because I've already found him. I want you,
Greg. Only you."

He took a deep breath, already stiffened from the
inside out, ready to tell her in very certain terms why
that wasn't an option.

Jedi nudged his hand at the same time Wendy's
finger gently covered his lips.

"However it looks," she said. "I don't need a perfect family. I need *our* family. Whatever that means.
If it's you, living here, and me in Spring Forest…
I'll do it, but I'll keep asking for more. If it's us here,
with you locked away from me in a separate room
when you sleep, then it's that. If the only kids you'll
allow yourself to have are of the canine variety, then
that's what we'll have…"

His eyes pooled with tears he couldn't deny.

"You and I both know there are no guarantees in

life. But we also know that your family will be there, backing us up, no matter what challenges present themselves, just as we'll be there for them. I mean, we're both pretty much the best at serving others, right? So why not ourselves? And a family of our own?"

He was about to bust wide open. Had to tell her to stop.

But her finger was on his lips again, and he wasn't strong enough to move it away.

Or step away.

"You can't ask me to step out and risk everything if you aren't willing to do it yourself."

He blinked. Her finger finally moved, freeing him to speak…but he had no rebuttal.

Because she was right. Everything she'd said. About what she wanted, but about his family, too. Who they were, what they were. What they did for each other.

And if his parents could stay in a dead bolted part of his house…or if a dog could eventually prove that Greg could fall asleep without the possibility of becoming brutal…but even if that couldn't happen… the dead bolted part of his house with his bed in it… locking him away from the house filled with a wife and kids…a dead bolted door that only closed late at night after the kids were tucked in and he'd held his wife until she fell asleep…

Life, people, weren't perfect.

But the most perfect love was staring at him out

of a pair of green eyes he couldn't escape. Didn't want to escape.

They'd beaten each other's walls down to their cores. All that was left was raw honesty.

And there was only one response coursing through him with a force he couldn't block.

In basketball shorts and a white sleeveless T-shirt, he knelt down with his good knee on the cobblestone walk and took Wendy's hand in both of his.

"Wendy Alvarez, will you—"

His left leg, having just come from a harder-than-normal workout gave a little. Jedi nudged their clasped hands. Hard.

And Greg stood up before he toppled over.

"Talk about imperfect moments," he said, but he was chuckling, clear to his bones. "I love you, Wendy. So much. I can't promise miracles, but I can promise that I will never willingly leave you. Will you marry me?" he asked the woman who'd brought laughter back to his soul.

Jedi nudged them again, and while he knew the dog could sense his tension, not understand his words, he amended, "Will you marry us?"

"Yep."

There was no hesitation in her voice. Just the plain speaking he'd come to trust. From the woman he adored.

Jedi barked. Wendy had tears in her eyes as Greg bent to give the love of his life a kiss filled with a lifetime of love, not just a moment.

"And oh, by the way, I love you, too," she said. "Both of you."

Jedi jumped up, his front paws on each of their arms. When he was working, that kind of behavior was not allowed, but for this moment as a young pup finding his forever home, his behavior was perfect.

The three wounded warriors had become a family.

* * * * *

Look for the next book in the
Furever Yours continuity,

A Double Dose of Happiness
by Teri Wilson
on sale July 2022

wherever Harlequin Special Edition
books are sold.
And catch up with the previous books in the
Furever Yours series:

Home is Where the Hound Is
by Melissa Senate

More Than a Temporary Family
by USA TODAY *bestselling author*
Marie Ferrarella

and

The Bookshop Rescue
by Rochelle Alers

On sale now!

#2917 SUMMER NIGHTS WITH THE MAVERICK
Montana Mavericks: Brothers & Broncos • by Christine Rimmer
Ever since rancher Weston Abernathy rescued waitress Everlee Roberts at
Doug's Bar, he can't get her off his mind. But the spirited single mom has no interest
in a casual relationship, and Wes isn't seeking commitment. As the temperature
rises, Evy feels the heat, too, tempting her to throw her hat in the ring regardless of
what it might cost her heart...

#2918 A DOUBLE DOSE OF HAPPINESS
Furever Yours • by Teri Wilson
With three-year-old twins to raise, Ian Parson hires Rachel Gray hoping she'll solve
all their problems. And soon the nanny is working wonders with his girls...and Ian.
Rachel even has him agreeing to adopt a dog and cat because the twins love them.
He's laughing, smiling and falling in love again. But will Ian need a double dose of
courage to ask Rachel to stay...as his wife?

#2919 MATCHED BY MASALA
Once Upon a Wedding • by Mona Shroff
One impetuous kiss has turned up the heat on chef Amar Virani's feelings for
Divya Shah. He's been in love with her since high school, but a painful tragedy
keeps Amar from revealing his true emotions. While they work side by side in her
food truck, Divya is tempted to step outside her comfort zone and take a chance on
Amar—even if it means risking more than her heart.

#2920 THE RANCHER'S FULL HOUSE
Texas Cowboys & K-9s • by Sasha Summers
Buzz Lafferty's "no kids" policy is to protect his heart. But Jenna Morris sends
Buzz's pulse into overdrive. The beautiful teacher is raising her four young siblings...
and that's *t-r-o-u-b-l-e*. If only Jenna's fiery kisses didn't feel so darn right—and
her precocious siblings weren't so darn lovable. Maybe it's time for the Morris party of
five to become a Lafferty party of six...

#2921 WHAT TO EXPECT WHEN SHE'S EXPECTING
Sutter Creek, Montana • by Laurel Greer
Since childhood, firefighter Graydon Halloran has been secretly in love with
Alejandra Brooks Flores. Now, with Aleja working nearby, it's becoming impossible
for Gray to hide his feelings. But Aleja's situation is complicated. She's pregnant with
IUI twins and she isn't looking for love. Can Gray convince his lifelong crush that he
can make her dreams come true?

#2922 RIVALS AT LOVE CREEK
Seven Brides for Seven Brothers • by Michelle Lindo-Rice
When a cheating scandal rocks Shanna Jacobs's school, she's put under the
supervision of her ex, Lynx Harrington—who wants the same superintendent job.
Maybe their fledgling partnership will make the grade after all?

**YOU CAN FIND MORE INFORMATION ON UPCOMING HARLEQUIN TITLES,
FREE EXCERPTS AND MORE AT HARLEQUIN.COM.**

HSECNM0522

SPECIAL EXCERPT FROM

HQN

Stationed in her hometown of Port Serenity, coast guard captain Skylar Beaumont is determined to tough out this less-than-ideal assignment until her transfer goes through. Then she crashes into Dex Wakefield. She hasn't spoken to her secret high school boyfriend in six years—not since he broke her heart before graduation. But when old feelings resurface, will the truth bring them back together?

Read on for a sneak peek at
Sweet Home Alaska,
the first book in USA TODAY *bestselling author*
Jennifer Snow's Wild Coast series.

Everything looked exactly the same as the day she'd left.

Though her pulse raced as she approached the marina and the nondescript coast guard station, her heart swelled with pride at the sight of the *Starlight* docked there. With its deep V, double chine hull and all-aluminum construction, the forty-five-foot response boat was designed for speed and stability in various weather conditions. Twin diesel engines with waterjet propulsion eliminated the need for propellers under the boat, making it safer in missions where they needed to rescue a person overboard. Combined with its self-righting capability to help with capsizing in rough seas, it had greater speed and maneuverability than the older vessels. The boat was the one thing she had total confidence in. And she would be in charge of it and a crew of five.

The crew was the tougher part. She was determined to gain their trust and respect. She was eager to show that she was one of them but also maintain a professional distance. Her father and grandfather made it look so easy, but she knew this would be her hardest challenge, to command a crew of familiar faces. People she'd grown up with, people who remembered her as the little girl who'd wear her father's too-big captain hat as she sat in the captain's chair in the pilothouse.

Did that hat finally fit now?

Weaving the rental car along the winding road, and seeing the familiar Wakefield family yacht docked in the marina, her heart pounded. The fifty-footer had always been the most impressive boat in the marina, even now that it was over thirty years old. Its owner, Kurt Wakefield, had lived on the yacht for twenty-five years.

Kurt had died the year before. Skylar peered through the windshield to look at it. Had someone else bought the boat? Large bumpers had been added to the exterior, and pull lines could be seen on deck. She frowned. Had it been turned into some sort of rescue boat?

It wasn't unusual for civilians to aid in searches along the coast when requested, but the yacht was definitely an odd addition. There had never been a Wakefield who had shown interest in civil service to the community...except one.

The man standing on the upper deck now, pulling the lines. Wearing a pair of faded jeans and just a T-shirt, the muscles in his shoulders and back strained as he worked and Skylar's mouth went dry. She slowed the vehicle, unable to look away. Almost as if in slow motion, the man turned and their eyes met. Her breath caught as familiarity registered in his expression.

And unfortunately, the untimely unexpected sight of her ex-boyfriend—Dex Wakefield—had Skylar forgetting to hit the brakes as she reached the edge of the gravel lot next to the dock. Too late, her rental car drove straight off the edge and into the frigid North Pacific Ocean.

Don't miss
Sweet Home Alaska,
available May 2022 wherever
HQN books and ebooks are sold.

HQNBooks.com

Get 4 FREE REWARDS!

We'll send you 2 FREE Books plus 2 FREE Mystery Gifts.

FREE Value Over **$20**

Both the **Harlequin® Special Edition** and **Harlequin® Heartwarming™** series feature compelling novels filled with stories of love and strength where the bonds of friendship, family and community unite.

HARLEQUIN

Heartfelt or thrilling, passionate or uplifting—Harlequin is more than just happily-ever-after.

With twelve different series to choose from and new books available every month, you are sure to find stories that will move you, uplift you, inspire and delight you.